Thomas Lake Harris

Regina

A Song of Many Days

Thomas Lake Harris

Regina
A Song of Many Days

ISBN/EAN: 9783744767217

Printed in Europe, USA, Canada, Australia, Japan

Cover: Foto ©Andreas Hilbeck / pixelio.de

More available books at **www.hansebooks.com**

REGINA:

A SONG OF MANY DAYS.

THOMAS L. HARRIS.

" MY SHEEP KNOW MY VOICE."

LONDON:

WILLIAM WHITE, 36 BLOOMSBURY STREET.

NEW YORK: NEW CHURCH PUBLISHING ASSOCIATION,
42 BLEECKER STREET.

1860.

To Stéphanie:

DOUBLY ENDEARED BY KINDNESS AND BY WORTH.

PREFACE.

I.

In ancient ages, glorious and golden,
  The Muse inspired: the Poet saw and sung;
But now, in sensuous thrall the spirit holden,
  Forgets the music of its native tongue.

II.

Yet smiling May replaces chill December:
  Again the vocal roses bud and bloom,
While hearts, with inner consciousness, remember
  The Lyric Heaven sublime above the tomb.

III.

Strike the heart's rock, ye thirsting sons and daughters!
  Strike it with Faith's unseen, immortal rod:
Anew will flow the sweet Castalian waters,—
  The true nepenthe from the wells of God.

IV.

Great Heaven o'erflows with brilliant inspirations,
   Vast as bright morning o'er the hill-tops gray;
And with us walk the beatific nations
   For Guardian Angels of our pilgrim way.

V.

Press on and fear not! let thy spirit's travail
   Bring forth a Life, inspired with the divine:
All mysteries their cloudy vail unravel,
   When, in the heart, celestial graces shine.

VI.

Forsake the slavish thrall of dead Tradition;
   Esteem the letter for the Spirit's worth:
Be this the burden of thy soul's petition,
   God's heavenly kingdom realized on earth.

VII.

So shalt thou know the glorious inner meaning
   Of Nature's poem, and the Lyric Word,
Clusters of blessedness in rapture gleaning
   From the celestial garden of the Lord.

INTRODUCTION.

—

Deep in this verdant hollow let me rest:
The evening sky in lovely red is drest
As if 'twere crimsoned from a young bride's face ?
Twilight trips by with her most quiet pace:
The butterfly and bee have gone to bed,
And the bold night-moth sips where flowers have shed
Their last perfection : Placid Wharfe afar
Breathes her pale mist in love toward the star,
Not loud, as when the boy of Egremound
Paused midway, trembled in the fatal bound,
And in the Strid sank to his dying swound ;
Then, waking on celestial lilies, found
A young lamb cropping by him for the hound.

The happy fairies from the fox-glove bells
Waft to mild Eve their delicate farewells.

Ah me! how sweet yon budding rose-tree smells;
Not rarer are immortal asphodels.

Dull sleep begone! the brown-winged beetles play
With drowsy murmur from the unmade hay:
The dreaming black-bird pipes his wistful lay,
"I know there are red cherries on the spray;"
Cherries for him and nectared fruits for me,
By green-capt fairies served on bended knee:
I feast as princely as the honey bee,
While a small elf, too small for eyes to see,
Sails by and winds his low-voiced melody:

SONG.

I.

Where the rose-tree buds unbar,
Where the purple pansies are,
Where the crimson wildings play
With the last-blown mountain May,
Fairies all are glad and gay.

II.

Blooming in this lucent light
Shine the graves in fairy white:

Angels, erst of lowly lot,
Sanctify the holy spot,
Hermits by the age forgot.

III.

Where the snowy owlet sails,
Where the tender gloom prevails,
From the crypt of ages old,
Lyric wine of amber gold
Flows for thee, O poet bold!

IV.

Holy men of long ago,
Come, with faces all a-glow.
Underneath the fretted stones
Pale Tradition sleeps and moans;
But above are angel-tones.

It is the sweetest night that ever fell;
And, as the young bird that forsakes its shell,
Thrilled by the ardors of the mother dove,
Who bosoms it with unextinguished love,
A Spirit Poem, Earth's delightsome guest,
Leaps to its life of music through my breast.

PRELUDE.

A crimson swan was falling through the air:
A leopard watched the bird, with hungry glare,
Until she lay expiring at his feet,
Then licked her blood and made her flesh his meat:
    Gorged on that dainty breast
He sank into a deep unconscious rest.

    The murdered swan arose,
Plumed with celestial brightness, from its woes,
And soaring sang melodiously till
The heavens were vocal. The Olympian hill
Peopled with gentle deities of old,
From its moist eyes the ancient slumbers rolled:
Goat-footed Pan upon his syrinx blew,
With music sweet as limpid honey dew:
All bashful wood-nymphs, hidden from the eye,
Breathed in their dewy rest deliciously:

Great Homer heard it, as blue mists **that rise**
From Helicon, the songs of centuries
With cloudy incense gathered in his brain,
Then melted into wreaths of silver rain :
From farthest Ind twelve dusky maidens came,
And with their subtile songs like nectared flame,
And calm reposeful **faces all** a-glow,
They budded into fruit-trees in a row,
Pouring sweet odors o'er the laughing earth :
Henceforth of poetry there was no dearth :
    A Golden Age began
To pant unborn within the breast of man.

    An Arab **on his** steed
Saw the fierce leopard on the red swan **feed,**
    And thrust a javelin
Into **its** brain : the beast began to spin,
Whirled in the death-dance ; and he cried, " Behold
This **mighty** pard, methinks, was over-bold
The bird of heaven within his maw to fold :
Now he is slain and feeds the humid mould."

Then, **from** the leopard's body, grew a tree :
So great was it that on its branches three
The Spring, the Summer, and the Autumn fed,

And slept beneath till all the leaves were shed.
Soon Spring awoke and hung the branches tall
With green and crimson garlands deathless all;
The smiles from out her laughing eyes became
Orblets and coronals of floral flame:
Then, like a maiden coy, she hid the globes
Of her white bosom in the dewy robes
Of the tree's exhalations; flying far,
As a moth flutters to the Evening Star.
Then Summer woke: the tree began to sing:
The piping blossoms saw him like a king;
He clapped his hands; from every floral nook
The spirits of the atmosphere forsook
Their deep seclusion; at his call the dew
In all the clusters to ripe fruitage grew,
And there were nectarines with golden spots,
And purple grapes, and crimson apricots,
And crisped love-apples red, and white as snow,
And luscious pears, and fruits the tropics know
The Sybarite, who sought for his repose
A bed of sweets without one crumpled rose,
Contented might have lived for ages there,
Nor cloyed his taste on such delicious fare.
Then Autumn wakened, with his staff in hand,
And shook the tree's full plenty o'er the land.

I asked the meaning of the parable
And took this answer, " Paradise is full
Of golden-breasted birds, who, like the swan,
Drop down from horizon to horizon;
And these are melodies, that have their birth
In far Elysium, but descend to earth.
The inner mind of man with hunger spies
The jewelled bird fly from its paradise,
And feeds upon it: so all poets are
Nursed in their souls with songs from heaven afar.
     Deep in the dreaming brain
The rising melodies their wings regain.

" The Lyric **of the** Morning Land was given
Thus-wise, and so the Starry Song of Heaven.
To feed the craving spirit they were sent,
And soothed it with an infinite content.
The Golden Lyric then came flying down,
And that young cygnet robed in yellow down
The sweet Odora; you have blest mankind
With music from the skies, but they are blind.
Yet rise with me and leave this burial ground:
Apollo sends you greeting.   Swift as sound
Or light that leaves the Pole Star, we will go
And stand before him."

This one spake, and lo!
I was translated o'er an Hellespont
Of starry circles. Like a pearly font
At some high altar, where the awful shrine
Is rich with pictured glories all divine,
A little pool of silence in my breast
Bubbled to song, and I was more than blest.

Now the great parable began to break
In meaning on my spirit, and I spake,
"King of the Lyric Heaven alone is He
Who bore the anguish of Humanity:
His poet-thoughts, like swans of crimson fire,
Circle melodiously through the gyre
Of threefold heaven, then, where to earth they fall,
Responsive souls absorb their essence all;
But in the heart they take a second life,
Then, through the mind, with visioned splendors rife,
Unfurl bright wings of poesy again
And from the lyric lips unvail to men.

"One musk grain scents for centuries a room;
One poem fills long ages with perfume.
Joy is immortal; sorrow weeps away
Like the last snow-drift from the lap of May.

A new-born Lyric is a bliss begun ;
Her laughing eyes outshine the summer sun ;
She clasps the earth as 'twere a rough cocoon,
Then leaps to life the wingéd Psyche soon.
I was a poet, waiting, Lord, to be
Changed from a leopard to a fruitful tree :
Thy songs became articulate in me.
Dead to the false I am, but, through the old
Dissolving selfhood, as it turns to mould,
One of the trees of heaven, with branches three,
Unfolds and blossoms to eternity.

"I am a dryad, and my limbs overflow
With juicy life ; the starry heavens, that blow
Like some blue lotus thickly set with gold,
Rain odors on me : In my buds I fold
The fruitful germs of melodies untold,
Nursed in my heart like new-born heroes bold.
There Ajax thunders with a long refrain :
Rhea and Saturn all their life regain.

"My name is Plenty ; all my branches bend
With dropping clusters, free to every friend.
My name is Mystery : where Music fails,
Where Poesy her broken wing bewails,

Where Life bows down within her sable shroud,
Or mourns her phœnix lost beyond the cloud,
Where dim Conjecture drops the final thread
And gropes among the mummies of the dead,
I lift my blossoms, wet with morning dew,
And bloom where Eden stood when Earth was new.

INVITATION.

I.

The Night her golden lamp has lit :
   Through Sleep's enchanted hollow,
She bids us trace the light of it :
   Come, follow me, O follow !

II.

Perchance thou shalt thy true love find
   Within some thymy hollow,
With Guardian Graces soft reclined :
   Then follow me, O follow !

III.

Perchance thou shalt thy youth regain :
   Though Earth is cold and hollow,
I know a charm for every pain :
   Then follow me, O follow !

IV.

There Dian bends her silver bow,
   And, in the dreamy hollow,
Endymion sleeps his joys to know :
   Then follow **me,** O follow !

V.

The Lady Moon her bosom dips
   Into that fragrant hollow;
Drink slumber from her dewy lips :
   Then follow me, O follow !

VI.

With morning **in their lucid eyes,'**
   Dwell, in that shady hollow,
The virgins of the lyric skies :
   Then follow me, O **follow.**

VII.

The dappled dawn shall newly wake
   Beyond the mystic hollow :
The ringdove murmurs in the brake :
   Come, follow me, O follow.

VIII.

The swelling buds forsake the tree
　　And blossom in the hollow,
But heart and mind shall bloom for thee:
　　Then follow me, O follow!

Into the land where Silence dips his urn
In still nepenthe from the soul's repose,
And pours it forth in honeyed thoughts, that burn
With liquid sweetness to consume thy woes;
Where his soft flute the shepherd Morning blows,
And yokes the amorous turtles to his car;
Oh follow! to the Heaven of the Rose;
Rise from Earth's visionary scenes afar,
In music led to meet the soft Luteian star.

Over the sunset seas, over the sunset seas,
Where the day has gone and the evening breeze,
Where the stars like naiads their bath forsake
In the lucid depths of the sky's blue lake,
And, vailed in the beams of their golden hair,
Rise to the surface and whisper there!

Into the Past, into the Past,
Where the Kings of the ancients their gems have cast;

Where Time, the great fisher, has thrown his nets,
And gathered the spoil that the World forgets;
Where all that hath been in its glory still
Is a palace of gold on a sapphire hill.

Into the Past, into the Past,
Where the year-drops fall and dissolve at last;
Where Life, like a rainbow with silver rim,
Is set o'er Eternity's ocean dim;
Where the prime in the present conceals its charms
As the old moon fails in the young moon's arms;
Where the dreams return that on earth were fed
By the lips long ago to the Angels wed;
Where the clouds all shine that have wept to rain;
Where the trees all bloom that are dust again;
Where all that hath been is a bridal night
Of whispers and kisses and soft delight,
That, wrapt in the sound of its last low tone,
Floats in the shadow beneath God's throne!

Into the Past, into the Past,
Where the luminous shadow of being is cast;
And the Centuries rest, when their toil is done,
Like giants who slumber at setting of sun;
Where the thoughts of all thinkers, if holy and true,

Dissolve in a mist-rain of morn-litten dew;
Where the loves of all lovers, if faithful and good,
Make one music for ever like leaves in a wood;
Where the tender and fond and the innocent-wise,
Like a pearl in the depth of the ocean that lies,
Have melted their being in silence away,
Come, **follow**! come, follow! beware of delay.

Where Music claps her hands in glee
And dances in the hollow,
Come shake the castanets with me:
Come, follow me, O follow!

Pour forth upon the earth thy song's oblation:
Lift up thy beaker to the constellation
That holds the star **Orion** in its hand:
Pursue the path of utmost Morning Land:
Apollo calls and the immortal **band.**
The spirit of the Lyric Sun respire.
Rise, living **spark**, from earth's consuming brand!
Soul, born of God's own essence, mount, aspire,
Nor falter at the path that Seraphim desire.

REGINA:

A SONG OF MANY DAYS.

OVERTURE.

IN a city of the Earth-world lived a Poet, in his prime,
He had won by ceaseless labors many praises of the time,
Striving ever, in the selfhood, through the wild world's
    battle storm,
To arouse the trampled nations to the combats of Reform.
He had watched by many death-beds and had mused by
    many graves,
He had seen the strong grow tyrants and the weak and
    poor made slaves,
But a deathless thought was in him and he bade its flame
    aspire;
It was this, that Heaven is nearer to the son than to the sire,

That a better day is coming, when the nations will unite
In the Brotherhood of Peoples, in the Commonwealth of
    Right.

Like a dying gladiator, who must battle to the last,
Words of hope and cheer he uttered though the life was
    failing fast,
Till a mighty Angel shivered, with his strong right hand,
    the glass
Of his Fancy's cloudy palace and its dome of burnished
    brass :
Then he fell to earth despairing, while a pulse of inner
    breath
Faintly quivered through the bosom in the bitterness of
    death.
For long nights of mortal anguish, like a martyr who has
    lain
Breathing on mid reeking corses where the jackals tear
    the slain,
He was trampled till Derision made a by-word of his toil ;
He was numbered with the fallen, he was counted with the
    spoil.

Visions of Messiah's glory passed before him as he lay,
Till within the awful Morning lit the poor down-trodden clay,

And it felt the breath eternal, while a second life began
To unfold a shrine within it for the coming Son of Man.
Then the form rose, slowly moving, all its heart and mind
     a-glow,
With the anthem sung by Angels eighteen centuries ago :
In their mystic tongue he chanted songs, that, inly under-
     stood,
Made the demons blanch and tremble in their war against
     the good,
While the sweet celestial music, as it echoed from afar,
Seemed the birth note of the day-spring or the bride song
     of a star.

He had known earth's hollow praises and had cast them
     under feet;
He had smiled with Faith and Duty in Affliction's furnace
     heat;
He had bled for others' sorrows and had toiled for others'
     needs :—
" Now," the solemn Angel whispered, " lay aside thy
     withered weeds;
Clothed in pure effulgent raiment lift thy golden harp and
     stand
With the priests, at God's high altar, in the deathless
     Upper Land."

Then the Book of Life was opened and the poet heard
     therein
Truths **to awe the drunken** nations in their carnival of sin ;
And he bore **to** earth a censer from the temple of the **Word,**
All whose living coals were burning with the Spirit **of the**
     Lord !

What availed the poisoned **arrows?** what the critic's ser-
     pent knife ?
Every wound a fountain opened **from** a deeper source **of**
     life ;
While the blows, in rich vibrations, like the hammer on **a**
     bell,
Set the inner chimes a-ringing of Messiah's love that tell.
All the losses **and** the crosses as he bore them turned to
     gains,
And he gathered grapes in clusters **from** the fruitage of his
     pains.
So the miracle was finished : **ere his** noonday was begun
He had seen the Lord transfigured, as the skylark views
     the sun;
And his life was merged in uses, as the fruit stalk when it
     dies,
Yet springs up to golden harvests for **the** reaping of the
     skies.

REGINA:

A Song of Many Days.

———

WITH jasmine blossoms in her hair,
And heart exhaling incense rare,
And smile the atmosphere that fed
With living sweets, and airy tread,
Holding a jewel of the sun,
Of all her sex the paragon,
Like sunset in its crimson flame
Through dying day the Vision came.

No peri of an Eastern tale,
No spectral phantom void and pale,
Nor empty unsubstantial ghost,
Nor dream from Fancy's mirage coast,
Yet like an apparition, lent
From Glory's boundless firmament,

In form an Angel, soul a child,
The **lovely** maid approached **and** smiled.

Her presence lit the dusky air;
  A jewel **from the** breast of dawn
Gleamed on her forehead, shining there .
  As if some cherub-hand **had** drawn
A wreath the temples to embrace,
  Blazing with lustre all its own,
And in the frontlet's burning space
  Inscribed Messiah's name alone.

She was a daughter of the Isle,
  Whose charms Apollo's bards rehearse,
Luteia* called :—its tender smile
  Bedecks our **own** sphered universe.
'Tis a white pearl amid the stars
  That necklace round **the Lady** Night,
Between the ruby planet Mars
  And Jupiter's pure **chrysolite.**

  * **The star** Luteia is presupposed, throughout the poem, to be an Asteroid, one
of the group revolving between Jupiter and Mars. This orb was peopled sub-
sequent to the **destruction of** the vast planet called in **this** Book "Oriana,"
where the moral **evil** of the universe had its origin, and which was consumed
by fire. Luteia **is** named in commemoration of the Poet of the Fallen Star, who,
withstanding the evil might of his brother Lucifer, **the** prince of demons, fell
a victim to his wrath, and was the first martyr; of which more in the sequel.

But in her eyes' mysterious light,
    As planets break from ocean rest,
A wonder met and awed the sight,
    And thrilled with Heaven's own touch the breast.
She charmed the Minstrel with her look,
    And laid within his open hand
The spirit of a living book,
    A blossom from Luteia's land.

"A queen I am," she said and smiled,
    "By right of inmost love alone;
My planet shines, a little child,
    Or baby's budding heart unblown:
Thought blossoms like the summer grain;
    We reap the harvests of the sea;
Our ocean land is all a plain
    Of undulating melody.
Haste to our mild delicious home,
    Where Nature is a jewelled robe,
That gleams like sunlit ocean-foam,
    Or pulses round the conscious globe.
Bright are the wells in human eyes
    Where Truth, the bridegroom, sees the bride;
Our orb is gemmed by fairer skies
    Where nobler beams of morning bide.

I will **a realm to thee unvail**
   Where substance is the slave **of** mind,
Where sin has left no trace of bale,
   Nor sorrow cast a shade behind.
Shrine in **thy** soul's interior sense
   The joy, the beauty, and the power,
To reach thy race with **life** intense,
   And charm them from **the** heavenly bower."

   I heard the words as hearing not :
   So the tired **fisher in his cot**
   Lists **the** wind whisper from the south,
   And feels **her** kisses on the mouth.

And then again melodious I heard,
As when the south wind, like some mighty bird,
Shakes from his wings the new-born April rain,
While the great streams their liberty regain.
Louder and clearer through my **listening** soul,
In measured strokes of melody and rhyme,
Came the white song-barge ; half from Earth's control
I rose into **a** vision all sublime.

Time stood and spake, " This man belongs to me
   By the red blood and by the body's fire ;

He journeys, in a little argosy
  Of music, round his planet in a gyre.
Grim Plutos hath not of his coming heard
In Hades, and sweet Mother Earth, unstirred
By rude hands turning up reluctant mould,
Doth not his coffin in her entrails hold.
His whirling atoms in their body spin
  With my diurnal motion : he is shaken
By day and night, my cymbals, in their din ;
  Nor hath his corse my treasure-house forsaken."

Then came Eternity ; and by him stood
A huge white war-steed, fetlock-deep in blood,
And all caparisoned in such array
As monarchs jewel for their crowning day :
High o'er his arching neck and visage proud
Twelve matchless rainbows in their vault were bowed,
And underneath his royal feet they met.
A slender maiden, with a coronet
Blazing above her calm pellucid face,
Held the strong charger spell-bound by her grace.

Now shone a second steed, as like the first
As are two mornings by one Summer nursed,
And, vaulting to my seat, I cried, Old Time,

D

Think'st **thou to** hold me from my natal clime?
Guard thou my body to the soul's return :
Impatient for the skies, I burn! I burn!

Time heard me, and replied, "Thou shalt not go!"
But from the dust, with many an ache and throe,
Clinging **to** that wild war-steed, I was borne
Beyond **dim** Earth, while, **into** pennons torn,
Its meteor flag was flying far **below.**
The maiden at my right began to glow
With sunrise : her delicious glances lent
To that vast pathway a divine content :
My spirit's rose-tree opened flower by flower.
Like morning, brightening through a thunder shower,
In splendid pomp of lightning veined with gold,
Her Spirit through my cloudy being rolled
Beauty, intense beyond all human flame ;
Then **on her** brow I read the Planet's name.

She whispered, **in** a pure celestial tongue,
"There is a Virgin Star, for ever young,
For ever beautiful, for ever wise,
And in its heart a little island lies
Where I must guide thee : 'tis my natal spot :
Each soul is there a Summer garden plot

Without a single seared or blighted fruit:
There unborn evil is for ever mute.
O* Poet, clasp thy sister's hand, for we
Are Lyric Angels of the same degree.
My spouse, my beauteous children round me stand
In that far palace, while my thoughts expand
Through budding stars, like fruit trees in a row,
To Earth, where thou a spirit-lance didst throw
At the fierce tyrants of thy human kind:
And lo! we will unitedly unbind
Sweet songs, that, when the kings of Earth bewail
Their dying empires, and the driving hail
Of anarchy and madness and despair
Bids the dark Titans for their doom prepare,
Shall melt upon the lowly with a thrill
Of inmost bosom-rapture, while the still
Unbounded peace of Heaven shall wake the eyes,
To hail the dawn of coming Paradise."

---

* The Lady Regina, called here a Lyric Angel, and also a spirit and a queen upon the terrestrial star Luteia, is in reality a royal matron of that orb, in whom the lyrical genius flowers to intense perfection. Her visitations and pilgrimages, through natural space and through the Heavens, are effected by the elevation of the spirit into the discrete degree above Nature, in which condition she is free to follow her divinely-given inspirations. So St. John, on Patmos, though surrounded by the scenery of that rude isle, in spirit beheld Heaven opened and rehearsed the wondrous things therein.

Then, as we sped, this mystic tale she told
Of the twelve planets in the days of old.

MERCURY.

Twelve children sat beside a silver urn :
Each found its fate.   The first drew skies that burn
With elemental genii, vast and wise.
This **was** the planet Mercury.   Her eyes
Dilated while the radiant gift unrolled :
Throned **on a** purple dais, fringed with gold,
She placed her sparkling hand within her breast,
And, in it, found twelve dovelets in a nest.
She breathed on these and each became a youth,
Burning at heart with ever-living truth.
The twelve then melted to a silver cloud,
And, underneath that jewelled sky, the proud
Imperial maiden saw them spring to birth,
And her young planet twinkled in its mirth.

She **whispered to the first, and** he shook out
Bright **wisdom-wings, and,** with a jocund shout,
Cleft the swift ether.   Trembling at his side
Floated his Athena, this was his bride.
Far to the south they built their bright pavilion,
Beneath a tree whose branches bore a million'

Mysterious flowers of star and sun and moon :
Each in its calyx folded a cocoon,
And, from their different but hallowed fire,
Came forth the fairies, and they formed a choir,
And multiplied and bred, till Silence grew
Pregnant with song.   The fruit-tree dropt its dew
In circling rays, that through the region spread
Where these young lovers in their prime were wed.

The married beams of the enamoured air
Gave birth to flowers that blossomed everywhere,
And, like sweet music, from an instrument,
The married odors of the flowers were sent
In pairs through all the gardens east and west,
Till every glade and grot their charm confest.

The married birds all day caressed each other,
And, as a sister tends her baby brother,
Heaven in its bosom cradled that young world,
And over it her vocal thoughts unfurled.

Then Night came forth, and from her artist hand
Frescoed the heavenly dome with visions grand
Of human Angels in their long-drawn state,
Marching in silence from God's palace gate.

All sciences, all arts, all pleasures were
Symboled in splendour through some wedded pair,
And each immortal drew its life confest
From the still rapture of All-father's breast.
Then, when the vaulted Pantheon was filled,
Through all in one the Word melodious thrilled
The burning conclave; while calm Night o'erleant
The restful orb as 'twere an instrument
Of music, and the vocal picture ran
Through spells and visions in the mind of man,
Who woke in spirit, from his vestments trod,
And in the Word received and worshipped God.

      So being came
      In beauty's flame,
Without a thought of human shame:
      The Orb of Will
      Began to thrill
With life of good devoid of ill.

VENUS.

The second drew a scimetar of flame
And in it shone the Lord Messiah's name:
'Twas Venus, second of the hosts of light.
Her visage grew unutterably bright;

Then in her breast she found a ruby key,
And oped with it the planet's destiny.
On sparry mountains with red fire a-glow
She dropt her mantle, white as driven snow;
Then rose a shepherd-people in its place,
Whose thoughts perfumed the air with subtle grace.
Then, lifting from her brow its coronet,
She found a city in the circle set,
Embowered in a paradise of trees
Whose deathless fruits with incense fed the breeze,
And everywhere the liquid fragrance gleamed
With an aromal brightness many-beamed,
And where the waves in their full radiance rolled
Grew spires and towers of crystalescent gold;
Then, where her rapid eyes in their dilation
Centered swift beams, uprose a glorious nation,
The lyric Lords and Omniarchs of song,
Whose epic harmonies, divinely strong,
Were wrought in social systems wise and great.
Sublime beyond the planet's outer gate,
One stood, to guard the orb from sin and death,
Whom mortals call Jesus of Nazareth!

EARTH.

Third in its place arose the planet Earth:
She drew a pall: it was her lot henceforth

To wear it, and a Star by lightnings driven,
Grew black and vanished from its place in heaven,
And she fled, crying " Woe, ah, woe is me !''
For the star's ashes rained incessantly
A storm of fiery serpents, and they stung
Her bosom to its quick ; her heart they wrung.

Then Earth despaired, till, from her breast, she drew
A lion, to a little child that grew.
Robed in a disk of blood her orb began
Its mazy circuit, and the first-born man,
Stung by **a viper,** the infection gave
To his pale offspring : these all found a grave.

Then followed him a race of men who fought
With golden armour, by Messiah wrought,
Against the serpents for a little space :
But, after them, by slow degrees, a race
In whom the serpents made their venomed seat :
Fierce anarchs, nursed in their red passion-heat,
Ravened like tigers fed on human spoil :
Then, as a lamp that pales for lack of oil,
The flickering planet floated, as a ghost
Borne meteor-like above Perdition's coast.

Some tossed their thoughts **as** foambells on a billow ;

These were philosophers, who, on the pillow
Of midnight speculation lit their dreams ;
Like glow-worms, pilotless, adown the streams
Of Nature they were drifted to their doom,
While their thoughts died as larvæ in a tomb.
There too were planet-readers, who the dim
White ether traced, but heard not the full hymn
Of joy and love and wonder, that awakes
When Night with starry hand her timbrel shakes.
And there were hierophants, whose hearts were wed
To demons, thrice accursed and inly dead,
Who on the image of Messiah trod,
Worshipped the beast, and made their passions god.
Earth was a centipede with flamy rings ;
A flying serpent clad with fiery wings ;
An asp against pure Heaven that reared its crest
As the worm struck at Cleopatra's breast ;
A steel-blue poinard in Perdition's grip ;
A pirate crew upon a merchant ship ;
A bridge of sighs above a venomed pool ;
A crownless king sunk to a painted fool ;
A reckless gamester, who his soul has cast
Against Despair and lost the stake at last.

There too were lovers, who their pale lips prest

Against Despair's white face and were at rest,
Then, linked in spirit, floated, partly born,
Like white clouds hovering 'twixt night and morn,
Toward their new birth-place. There were children small,
Who gasped on Earth, or scarcely breathed at all;
Yet they were deathless : o'er Misfortune's power
Each rose, a perfume from a broken flower ;
They fluttered heavenward in their stainless pride,
Like sighing love-words from a murdered bride,
Or prayers from one whose life exhales away
In gentle mercy to the closing day,
Or kisses pressed upon the lip at even
But whispered in devotion's breath to Heaven,
Or the still night-scents that the dawn exhales,
Or the star's lustre when the cloud prevails,
Or pure March violets that a young wife's hand
Culls from the snow to grace her bosom-land.

There too were infants never seen by man,
Who died before their breathing life began :
Earth's corpse-lamps flickered not to pain their eyes ;—
The white light pales before their whiter skies,
The white ray trembles into dusk before
The pearly day-star twinkling at their door ;
For in their veins the red blood scarcely grew,

And they were fed on antenatal-dew
Where silver planets shook melodious rain
Upon them through the mother's beating brain :
These all were nursed in Heaven's serene seclusion,
Unshadowed by the World's malign illusion :
These in the snow-white tents of being bide :
Their lucid thoughts,—pure as the pillowed bride
Seen by the night lamp's, dim and shadowed ray,
Pallidly beautiful, dissolve away
In silence, sweet as kisses are in dreams,
When parted lovers meet, beside the streams
Of youth and morning, and their souls are cast
In Hymen's crucible and fused at last.

The night-moth flutters to the silver moon ;
The night-blown jasmine floats, in pale perfume,
Intense beyond all fragrance, to the stars,
Ere hooded Morn the dappled east unbars.
Clear Phosphor, on his couch of lucid snow,
Slumbers entranced ere day's red roses glow ;
So these pure Naiads of the wells of time
Without a name pass to their gentle clime :
Fair flowerets, rooted never in the sod
Of Mother Earth, but, like great Aaron's rod,
Endowed with mystic power to part the sea
Of outer life, they find eternity.

The little nuns, safe cloistered from the tomb,
Grow in God's time to hymeneal bloom.
These are the snow-drops, blossoming in state
Beyond eternity's perpetual gate :
These are the diamond pendants in the ears
Of the Queen Heaven ; the windfalls of the years
Ripened above : their tiny hands have prest
The globes of life in Heaven's impassioned rest.
And some are poets there ; they muse apart,
In trances blossoming, where Heaven's deep heart
Glides into sound around them, and are still,
Till from its perfectness they drink their fill.
They cleave the air in gondolas of fire,
Each lifting far aloft a seven-stringed lyre,
With tuneful chords by the heart's rapture fed,
And, from the lyres, white plumy wings are spread
Which undulate with music ; they are driven
In their song's motion to intensest Heaven.

Where their still feet press the pellucid streams
Of ether, bloom sweet flowers, that whisper dreams,
And blend their life with air, as kisses lie
On fragrant lips and in that fragrance die :
And there are floating pictures, which they glass
In silent oceans that they overpass,
Where color is forgotten, for the light

Sways its own beams as Dian rules the night,
And shapes them into images which walk
In vails, transparent as melodious talk
Of friend with friend, when each the heart lays bare,
And Truth is throned in her own temple there.

As dewy Sunrise gathers in her hand
The floating mist, and weaves it, in a bland
Moist coronal, about her beamy brow,
These gentle poets with their thoughts endow
The harmonists, who pile their massive weight
Of thunder-songs against the planet's gate.
Their souls are islands in the lyric sea:
Each is a hive whose bees of melody
Suck fragrance from the flowers God's hand hath sown
Through the wide Heaven's illimitable zone:
But other poets love them, as the bowers
Love the sweet spirits that were not quite flowers,
And lull them tenderly, with music deep,
Till, in their souls, blue Day begins to peep
Through orient sapphires, with a dulcimer,
Calling her artist band to follow her.
Then Dawn, like Titian, sets his thought a-glow,
And paints the Sunrise on their fields of snow:
Then Eve, like Claude, above the meadows low

Hangs the young moon, white as a lily blow,
Trembling upon the Sunset's crimson towers,
And opes the stars, like silver lotus flowers,
On the blue Ganges of the holy skies.
Or Noon, that Michael Angelo, with eyes
That in their spectrum hold the brightness cast
Upon his face when God Messiah passed,
With Rafaelle scarfed in crimson at his side,
And Turner in his art-dream glorified,
Holds the bright palette 'gainst the blazing dome,
And paints the Day-spring in her heavenly home,
Where every color, in its element
Of Love and Wisdom interfused and blent,
Runs through celestial spheres its radiant race,
And finds in God an everlasting place.

There, gliding in a dream, so calm and holy,
That evermore mild-minded Melancholy
Seems, in their shadow, to forget the dearth
Of poesy and gladness in the earth,
And half unlearns herself in blisses new
And strange to her, as skies of summer blue
To winter buds or wind flowers, that awake
Beneath dark fir-trees in some northern brake,
Delicious beams from every orb they borrow,
That shines above the atmosphere of sorrow :

They dance with the sun,
In the rays that run
Through the tuneful realms of space,
And ascend, in the might
Of their young delight,
To the Father-Mind's embrace.

SONG OF ORIONA.

She was no vapor of the night,
Lost in a dream at morning light;
No momentary shadow, sent
To be a day's astonishment;
No phantom from the spheres below
With influence of bale and woe.

Her dimpled hands, her snowy feet,
Her lips with Hymen's honey sweet,
The wedded roses on her brows,
Betokened a celestial spouse.
Soft floating in the perfumed mist,
While balmy airs her raiment kissed,
She whispered, " Lo ! on beamy wing,
A love-gift from thy Lord and King."

Then beckoned with her **jewelled hand,**
And drawing near from Hymen's Land,
A gleaming car of silver light,
That moved from some inwrought delight,
Borne o'er **the** pure, Elysian sea,
Approached and then stood still by me.

In it I saw a wingéd child
In robes of starlight soft and mild.
Upon the pure, seraphic face
The joys of Heaven had left their trace,
And on the brows, from sorrow free,
Were garlands of the jasmine tree.

" This child," the lady said, " is one
Whose outward life was not begun,
Ere, like a bud that's never blown,
It vanished from a world unknown."
Then, with a voice **more sweet and** low
Than songs that dreaming fairies know,
That heavenly child its hymn began,
While through my heart the music ran.

" Such as me, such as me,
In divine felicity,

Souls of infants, never born
On the dusky world forlorn,
Like the early cowslip, blow
Far beyond the grave-yard snow.

" On my birth no mother smiled ;
Father never owned me, child ;
On the earth I had no spot
E'en in memory's mystic grot ;
Mortal name I have not won,
Yet I shall out-last the sun.

" In bright Heaven's clear-shining fold
Millions, of a name untold,
Like the spirits of the flowers,
Bloom in life's eternal hours :
Forms on earth we never knew
Make us fair for Angels' view.

" When the Lord, upon the cross,
Won the earth from bale and loss,
And His human grew divine,
From His heart the mystic wine
Fashioned forms for children small,
That they might be Angels all."

E

Bring me the harp that King Apollo strook :
My soul is sitting in a cloistered nook,
Bowered in orchards ; all their spices fail
In dying kisses on me, while the pale
White moon is rising, calmly as the mild
Departing spirit of an unborn child :
I think I am an Angel white as snow ;
My lily-bud of life begins to blow.

" **I was, on** Mother Earth, an infant small,
And, mutely as the feathered frost-flakes fall,
Slid from **its** sorrows ere I left the womb
Thy little daughterling began to bloom
Beyond **the narrow** threshold of the **tomb :**
They call **me** Oriona where I dwell,
In a small islet, where the white waves tell
Their endless joy in Music's faintest tongue,
Is my abiding-place ; Time is so young !
He plays with us like **Cupid with** his doves :
We drink the honey-dew that morning loves,
And **in great golden** flowers, where merry elves
Delight **their babes** to nurse, we hide ourselves,
And deck **the** ringlets of our gleaming hair
With aromatic blossoms floating there,
Born from the South wind's delicate embrace ;
But, when dim night holds you in lower space,

Our Angels bring us viewless to behold
The shapes you cherish in the dusty mould:
Then we are glad that we are not contained
In bodies rudely made and coarsely grained,
But free to rove at will through Heaven Divine
Like flambeaus in the hand of God we shine,
Blazing with such sweet fragrance that we cast
No shadow : when our heavenly youth is past
We grow to lordly shape and essence rare :
Our souls are pearls that Heaven delights to wear
Set in her argent splendors : in our eyes,
That never wept, shine the unfallen skies.

" We are of genius opposite to those
Who wither on the planet's blighted rose,
In threescore years of lingering heart distress.
Our little spirits, winged and pilotless,
Rise o'er death's dying flame triumphantly :
For us blind Sorrow gropes in vain, but we
Laugh in his wrinkled face, and borne aloft
On dewy clouds of incense warm and soft,
Are floated to Elysium, o'er the still
Sweet air that feeds us : like young grapes we thrill
Amid the vine leaves of our happy lot,
While on the earth men think that we are not.

And there are babies of a six-months' size :
The light of many stars is in their eyes :
The joys of many Heavens east, west and south,
Lurk in the kisses of the dimpling mouth :
Their festive souls are vocal all day long,
And in their minds, like fruit-trees of rich song,
Whose leaves are melodies, the ages old
Their deep translucent music-thoughts remould.
Grafts into king Apollo's garden trees,
   We grow to royal bloom, and are complete
In all our human lives and harmonies
   Of truth and virtue, and our days are sweet
With fruits of every season.   There are shed
Sweet love-rains on us, till our hearts are wed
To music's inmost person, whom ye call
Jesus of Nazareth : our souls are all
Love-mirrors, where His image multiplies
Itself as morning through uncounted skies :
We are the rainbows of His summer shower,
Trembling on sorrow's verge a little hour,
Then lifted from the earth-world's cloudy bar,
And wreathed around the Bright and Morning Star.''

—————

   The mystic song was o'er :
Lost in a dream of soul-dissolving bliss

I floated silently,
    In the diffusion of my elements,
    Above the peaceful sky
    And the reposing world ;
    And hope was in my heart,
    And love was in my soul,
    And music in my breath,
While mighty Expectation flew before
    With plumes of crimson flame.

Like flowers that bloom in some far wilderness,
    Unseen by mortal eye,
    To earthly minds unknown,
  The stars of an aromal universe
Breathed forth their lives in sweetness on the air,
    And gathered back their beams.
    Twelve planets far more dense
Rolled on their burning axles : in the midst,
   Like a vast golden island in a lake
   Belted with water-blooms of every hue,
    Shone the transparent sun.
Dante and Æschylus were by my side,
    And Milton with us there,
For all the good compose one family,
Nor youth, nor age, nor poverty, nor shame
Destroy the happy concord of their minds :

In the transfusion of accordant souls
The separate rivers of sweet melody
Flow to a lyric sea, pervading all.

Then like a castled city, which by night
Burns from a thousand minarets and spires,
 As if a maniac girl
Should wave white arms and chant insanely on,
Till her thin robes and dark dishevelled hair
 Kindled in lurid flames,
 Shone Earth amid the stars :
 But all beside was peace.

The smoke of that great burning, like a robe,
Floated in pallid ether; through it shone
The lonely isles and massive continents,
The gay, the proud, the strong, the worldly-wise
 Wrapt in a common doom ;
Yet each pursued his favorite phantasy,
As the expiring thoughts of one who dies
Crowd the aërial palaces of mind,
Then, lost in wild illusions, pass away.

 "This," cried an inward Voice
That spake in all the organs of the breast,
As sunrise kindles through a thousand isles,

Waking the dwellers there,
  " Is Earth's expiring hour :
From the transpicuous **ashes** she ascends
The wide cerulean, **floating, in** the beams
Of endless morning, to her goal, the skies.
One grape alone upon Heaven's vine is blighted;
One constellation only hath a star
  Whose habitants, affrighted,
Rush wildly to abysmal vales afar :
  All else is harmony.
  The universal space
Views but one stain upon its azure veil :
  The Upas tree of sin
Bears the death-apples for one orb alone.
  The serpent, Evil, coils
From one devouring darkness, only one.
One orb denies where all the planets pray,
And the meek suns pour endless orisons
  At God Messiah's feet."

——

Then I oped my mouth in sayings :
In my parable I gathered
Pearls of wisdom without number,
As the diver from the ocean,
And my soul-thought wafted earthward.

———

PARABLE OF THE MORNING. *of Earth Redemption*

Once the stars of night were fading
In the early morning paleness;
All the night birds sank to silence;
All the night flowers closed their petals;
All the night winds hushed their voices;
And the street lights, in the cities,
Flared and flickered and were darkened :
All the watchmen then grew silent;
Not a foot-fall smote the pavements;
Sick men, turning on the pillow,
Saw the night lamp slowly dying,
And **the** friendly watchers dreaming
In their places by the bed side.

In his tent the Warrior slumbered,
Dreaming o'er his deeds of battle,
Dreaming of the great true hearted
Who had fought and died before him.
In his cell the Priest, repeating
Creeds and aves without number,
Felt the numb words dropping slowly
On the frosted air, and slumbered;

Still a sleep, with doleful accents
Dropt the dead prayers, and was silent.

Then a white Swan, high in ether,
Saw the vision of the sunrise,
Floating in the skies' dominions,
Bathed his breast in golden splendor,
Bathed his wings in crimson brightness,
And he cried, " The sun is rising."
Then the cocks, in all the barn yards,
Woke and crowed a shrill denial;
And the frogs, in all the marshes,
Saw the Swan's wings slowly fading
In the far-off golden ether,
And they mocked in their derision
At the prophet of the morning.

All things on the earth were waiting
For the day-light and its wonders;
Mighty steamers for departure
To the land of gold and spices;
Rapid cars to cleave the distance,
Bringing far-off friends together.
Then a Skylark, slowly rising
Through the white mists of the valley,

Saw the Sun leap on his war horse,
Heard him thunder at earth's portals,
Saw him cleave the Giant Darkness,
While the gates of day flew open ;
And he rained his mellow music
Till a thousand happy voices
Echoed back " The sun is rising."

Brother mine, let Wisdom teach thee,
Lest thou too be found in slumber,
When the Good Man of the household
Calls his faithful ones before him ;
For the night is passed already,
And the Mighty One of Ages
Hath His hand against the portals :
We are living in the newness
Of the age wherein the nations,
In the balances of judgment,
Shall be tried by Him who cometh.
They are wise who wait His coming
With their hearts from sin uplifted,
With their lips who teach the blinded,
With their hands who raise the fallen,
With their hearts who bless the lowly,
Giving bread to those who need it,

And a cup of pure cold water
To the thirsty ones who perish.

He who standeth at earth's portals,
Leaping on His snow-white charger,
Like the day itself for brightness,
Is the Lord of earth and heaven.
Lo! He cleaveth down the darkness
And the world awakes to meet Him.
He is coming to the Warriors,
To the mighty of the people,
To the men whose hearts are courage,
To the men whose hands are valor.
He is coming to the Priesthood,
To the men whose hearts are mercy,
To the men whose hands are patience.
" Lo!" He crieth, " be ye ready;
I have heard you, O my people!"
He is coming to the tyrants,
To the nobles at their feastings,
To the proud ones in their splendor.
He is coming to the lofty,
Who have built their thrones to heaven.
He. is coming to the lowly,
Who have prayed, in secret places,

Lest their foes shall overhear them.
To the blind who have no teacher,
To the sick who have no healer,
To the weak who have no helper,
He is coming. Wrath and mercy
In His thunderbolts are blended.

Hear, while yet, a little longer,
Wisdom holds communion with thee.
Hear the lark-song that descendeth;
'Tis thy own heart, that hath risen
From the body's earthly portals,
In its faith and hope gone skyward.
Hear thy heart, the mystic singer!
"**Lo!**" it says, "the night is ended,
And the morning light is surging
O'er the sunken isles of darkness,
Bearing thrones upon its bosom
Like dead leaves before **the** billow."
Lo! the thunder-drum is beating
In the valley of the judgment.
Withered bones of Creed and Custom,
Shrivelled hands of worth departed,
Empty skulls of faith, that liveth
But in seemings and illusions,—

All are to their place returning:
Clad in grave-clothes they encumber
All the space beneath His presence:
Creeds on Creeds, a mighty legion,
Some with bodies all of serpents;
Some with twofold Janus faces;
Some with vipers in their bosoms;
Some with coils like anacondas;
Some with jaws like wolves or tigers,
Dripping with the blood of slaughter;
Some in robes of priestly purple;
Some in sable hue apparelled;
Some with armies marshalled round them;
Some with slaves who do their bidding;
Some with kingdoms bowed before them,—
Lo! they stand, as ripe grain standeth,
Circled by the reaping sickle.
Hear the war-horse, how he paweth!
Mark the death-flames in his nostrils!"—
'Tis the voice in thine own bosom
That is speaking this within thee.

Floating skyward, floating sunward,
The great mind of earth is bathing
In the brightness of the Coming.

Like a swan, with wings of crimson,
It is floating far above us.
Thus thy inner mind, O brother,
Far above the world is lifted.
" Lo !" it cries, " the day is breaking,
But the night,—that cometh **also** :—
Day for those who robe their spirits
In the vestal truth of heaven,
In the love of doing uses ;
Night for those who stand defiant,
Heedless of the calls of mercy ;
Mocking **at** the Lord above them ;
Crushing out the life within them ;
Treading down the poor below them."

SONG OF THE FESTAL FAY.

I.

Then in my heart a festal fay,
By angel-gift made inly nigh,
On pipe and tabor 'gan to play
" The Golden Age shall never die.

II.

" Let sorrow melt from every soul
    And **sunshine kindle in** the eye,
For Love regains its first control,
    The Golden Age shall never die.

III.

" Come praise the Lord with festive mirth,
    As Angels praise Him in the sky :
His gladness blooms for all the earth ;
    The Golden Age shall never die.

IV.

" With plenty smiles the jocund year ;
    The seasons ripen as they **fly** :
Respond to Heaven with songs **of cheer** ;
    The Golden Age shall never **die.**

V.

" **With** heart to heart and hand **to hand,**
    Mankind shall own Messiah nigh :
Their souls to angel-grace expand ;
    The Golden Age shall never die."

SONG OF CORONIS.

A child-like man of festive race
Sped by my side a little space ;
Coronis was the name **he bore** ;
He told these happy numbers o'er.

I.

There's gladness in the sister stars !
    Rejoice ! rejoice !
And Venus talks to crimson Mars,
    With blithesome voice.

II.

The Earth revives that once was slain !
    Rejoice ! rejoice !
And pipes anew her primal strain,
    With blithesome voice.

III.

The dancing Seasons in their glee,
    Rejoice ! rejoice !
The World's glad nuptials troop to see,
    With blithesome voice.

IV.

She bows at God Messiah's feet:
Rejoice! rejoice!
And finds her life in His complete,
With blithesome voice.

Upon our planet once lived men so holy
That, underneath their feet, the crimson moly
Blossomed, and overhead the mystic larch
And the tall pine-tree bent to wreathe an arch,
And leafy lindens shook their blossoms down
To form for them a wood-god's dewy crown,
And sighing poplars whispered sweet delight,
Changed in their genius by such gentle might.
These drew their being three parts from the air,
And one part from the essence, pure and rare,
Which wanders, when the fields begin to blow,
From hawthorn hedges through the meadows low,
And, mingled with the steamy breath of kine,
And with the budding cowslips' pearly wine,
Floats o'er the evening vapors and exhales.
Their other part is wafted by the gales
Of summer pleasure from some latticed star,
Remote in ether: These are wiser far

F

Then all the gentle souls who with them dwell :
They rest like fire-flies in a summer dell,
Poised o'er their planet's dim suffusive weather,
And floating thus, in low soft words together,
They talk of things which have been, but are not.
Like shrine-lamps burning in some lovely spot,
Steaming with fragrant oil, they twinkle still,
Drinking from antique flagons, which they fill
With songs that by the world are heard no **more,**
Great songs great poets grandly sung of yore,
When language was a fruit tree manifold,
Of crimson blossoms streaked with noonday gold,
And poetry and music, in their bliss,
Trembled together to their first sweet kiss.

Beautiful was the Past,

When Time, the baby, smiled
In the maternal Heaven's enamoured face,
And drank her sweet delight.
'Twas then these **poets lived,**
Feeding with melody,
Drawn from the organ stops of many stars,
In Nature's solemn instrument, the mind.
All was their heritage
Hid in the gentle wisdom of the flowers,

Whispered from leafy groves where Dryads dwell,
　　Or by low breathing Night,
　When lovers, in their dreams,
Glide hand in hand, to find their being's bliss
In happy isles where young immortals are.
　　We sped upon our way,
Through avenues instarred with grottos dim,
Formed from the crystals of their lyric thought,
　　And heard this mystic hymn.

HYMN OF THE NEW GOLDEN AGE.

I.

The Golden Age returns again,
Through troops of inly breathing men,
Who ope, with mild and glad surprise,
The thousand-gated harmonies.

II.

In still delight their pulses chime
To the Æolian harp of Time,
Upon the sands of space they tread,
With God's effulgence inly shed.

F 2

III.

They ask no thought from outward lore,
But brim the world with wisdom o'er;
And find, through Nature's dim disguise,
Celestial voices and replies.

IV.

In every wayside flower they scan
The wisdom of the Father-Man,
And, from the husk of custom free,
Enunciate Divinity.

V.

All that for ancient wisdom grew
For young experience blooms anew :
In orphic hymns through heart and brain
The meaning of the Word is plain.

VI.

Through every sun the path they trace
That brightens to the central space ;
And in the chiming blood-drops hear
The songs of every human sphere.

VII.

At life's great sacrament they thrill,
Receiving Christ in mind and will,

And, meekly patient of the base,
Reflect the lustres of His face.

More soft, more lowly, fell,
In pure deliciousness
Of fragrance wed to **melody, that stirred**
The fairies of the heart from their repose,
From Hesper's distant **orb,**
This joy-inspiring lay.

SONG OF THE VESPER ANGELS.

I.

Hark! the Evening Star is singing : you may hear **the**
numbers thrill
The deep soul-air with their **music while the** atmosphere **is**
still.
'Tis a song of many poets, many angels blent in one.
Hark! the mild melodious thunders that re-echo from the
sun.
Star by star the Night grows vocal : **like a lyre of many**
strings,
Nature wakes beneath His fingers while the Great Musi-
cian sings.

II.

Listen! listen! O thou spirit who from earth hast known
    and heard :
Soon the happy world shall waken to the music of the Word :
Men shall worship in the twilight, when the outward day
    is done,
While the Spirit east is lightened with the vast Angelic Sun.
They shall see the sky grow clearer, **till the golden flames**
    are bent
In a galaxy of glory round the blue and **starry tent.**

III.

Bright and brighter, in the God-light, shall the vault of
    Nature gleam :
Earth shall waken to the real from its dim delusive dream:
Earth shall waken, while the planets, like the buds on
    Aaron's rod,
All unfold their snow-white clusters, dropping music on
    the sod ;
Dripping spices, till the ether, as a spirit rose is sweet :
Then mankind shall kneel adoring at the God Messiah's
    feet.

IV.

Listen! listen! wave the slumbers from thy lucid eyes
    away ;

Fill thy soul with pure affections on thy love-delighted
    way,
For, in mystical white raiment, shall the saints at God's
    right hand,
In His presence all transfigured, journey on from land to
    land,
Felt in lowly human dwellings, when the light of day is
    dim,
With a breath of bosom fragrance, with a tender spirit
    hymn.

v.

They shall sing, till Silence wakens like a Naiad from her
    well ;
And the heart within the bosom, as it were a Sabbath bell,
Through the corridors of feeling, through the mind's
    eternal dome,
Pulses on with sweet vibrations of the blessed angel home.
O the rapture, O the glory, of the happy age to be
When the years with fruits are laden from the Heavens'
    immortal tree !

Celestial journeys are by change of state :
The happy spirit may be tranced away,

And consciously float o'er the body's bars,
Into the liberty of earth and sky,
Regaining its primeval heritage,
Sight, that through all the spheral universe
Traces the mazy circuit of the star.
And, kindling in the heart of things, makes known
That secret beauty which their forms declare.
Or swift, or slow, or through the dim obscure
Of dream-life, or the conscious waking thought,
And sight which is thoughts' minister, we glide,
Far as the Morning travels, when she moves,
A virgin Grace bent on her sweet employ,
Unfolding universes from the buds
Of world-germs by the Lord Messiah sown.

We sped by change of state through wondrous realms,
Into perception drawn of each as we
Inhaled the virtues of their vital air,
And so respiring drank their joy, and so
In joy received clear insight to behold
Their beauties, varying as lights that gleam
Through ocean rainbows in the early sun.

'Tis respiration that unfolds the mind
To astral knowledge, to the solar sphere

Is the religion of the Fairy world;
Nor can they ever fall away from this
But bloom and ripen with an infant's joy.

To the small fay man is a universe,
The brain a sun, the lungs a galaxy;
Man holds a constellation in his hand
Of fairy people, hymning in the tides
Of the red heart-life through the veins that flow.
All the fay kind within one human form
Are lifeless germs of being, till the Lord,
In His great second coming, animates
Their infant bodies : then they wake at first
As Adam woke in Eden, 'neath the tree
Of the soul's life, in whose ripe fruit they grew.
Within the breast they find a paradise,
And are the primates of their own sweet race.
As man becomes regenerate, in Love's
Inmost transfiguration, he puts on
Immortal newness : fairy families
From all the lungs, that inwardly inspire
In God Messiah's fulness, make their way
Throughout the frame's proportions, till, at last,
The body thrills instinct with fairy life,
While from each heart Messiah breathes His love.

The fairy world from Adam was withdrawn
Because he sinned; but inly breathing men
Who followed, in the world's first Golden Age,
Received the precious gift, till Love declined;
But when internal respiration ceased,
The fairy peoples of humanity,
Remote in woods, and fields, and dewy flowers,
Found homes within the human breast no more.

Moral disorders wrap the human mind
In fiery dream-clouds, which, to fairies, are
As battle-fields to us, where millions pour
Death-dealing horrors on infuriate foes.
The gentle fairies view the sight afar,
And veil their lucid eyes, and turn away;
But now they cry that "Christ, their Life, is come,
And they in glory are to reign with Him:"
The fay millennium dawns upon their sphere
When men first breathe from God Messiah's fires.

As the new Eden grows from heart to heart,
In our dear Lord's Divine Humanity,
The fay race gather, from Caribbean Isles
Or spicy groves of Indus and Cathay,
Or England's gardens, gay with varied bloom,

Or northern mountains rich with balmy pines.
Their ensigned hosts display, in burnished helm
And lances like the beams of happy eyes,
And surcoats woven as of bridal smiles,
Some peaceful counterpart of that great war
Which the regenerate in spirit know.

They haste to claim the pure wife's yielding breast,
Or build their homes within her tender eyes,
Or doubly consecrate the hallowed lips
And charm the soul with paradisal joy.
Then voice in voice and thought in thought and love
Insphered in love declare their blissful reign :—
Such life as this lost Eve, when paradise
With all its fairy people fled **away.**

Through respiration comes the power to find
The fay-life hidden in the vocal woods.
No tree **but is** the outwork of the fay,
As thus I sang where flows deep-bowered Wharfe,
In her white mist-robe, hermitess of Night,
'Neath Bolton's ruined shrines to kneel and pray.

THE WOOD FAYS.

The wisdom of the golden times,
 When Earth the child was young,
Flows round my heart in playful rhymes
 That heavenly maids have sung;
And I will weave a poem rare
 As music that is fed,
Where kisses laugh into the air
 From lovers newly wed.

Poesy, the dappled fawn,
In the lucid pools of Dawn
Bathes her lips with honey dew,
Ere to Heaven she bids adieu;
And the steaming mists, upcurled,
Slake the anguish of the world.

Virgin globes of breathing snow,
Move divine in Heaven I know;
Melody and rhyme! ye thrill
Where Apollo takes his fill,
Of the blisses deep that lie
In your pure tranquillity.

Lifted **from** the outward ken
Of the dim world's twilight men,
Gentle wood-nymphs, through the brake
Lead me, for the Muses' sake.
I would seek the dappled fawn
Drinking from the pools of Dawn.
I would find the lady sweet,
Thrilled within whose bosom-heat
Melody and meaning meet.

All the earth is now forlorn.
Poets find the lyric horn,
Quaffed **by wiser** ancients, dry.
But **I** know that in the sky
Sweeter vintage flows than **erst**
Fed great Homer's epic thirst,—
Vintage that if one could find
Would enchant the vocal mind.

From the leafy lindens tall,
From the arbor-vitæ small,
From the larch-tree and the plane,
While the evening winds complain,
Gather in your hidden grace,
Forms that painters die to trace.

Ere a seed can live and grow
Veiled in dusty earth below,
Gliding through their atmosphere
Fairy angels hover near.
In the germ its own bright fay
Wakens at the word they say,
Growing with a still delight,
Fed from Heaven by day and night.
Not a plant on earth is born
But is robe by fairy worn.
I have found your hallowed grot,
Hermit fays by man forgot.
What is Nature? it is all
Art-world of the fairy small.

In no cell of earthly rind
Is the dryad fay confined :
He may summon at his will
Comrades true his place to fill :
Gliding through the dewy leaves
He is glad, in Summer eves,
Jocundly to rise and sport
In blue ether, Fancy's court.

Gentle dryads, ye who drink
At the silver streamlet's brink,

I from earth would slip away,—
Poet-brother of the fay.
I have heard your brethren trill
Echoes to the whip-poor-will,
Where the mellow August moon
Floated o'er the waves of Schroon.
As we go we will unbind
Fairy songs upon the wind.
Give to me your airy grace;
Let me still the pathway trace
To the Lyric Sun's embrace
And Apollo's kingly face.

SONGS OF THE FAY.

I.

THE COURTING FAIRIES.

The Courting Fairies in the grass
  Awake their music all night **long:**
Sing heart, glad heart, and in the glass
  Of Faith survey the airy throng.

The butterfly her toilet makes:
  Look up, glad heart, the sight behold:

And **threefold** heaven. In his instinct wise
The fairy, hid within the buried seed,
Adores All-Father : in his act,—for prayer
Is union with the Infinite,—he opes
His tiny lungs, inspiring auras drawn
From the full bosom of Creative Bliss.
Trace then the constant miracle of bloom
To its beginning, and we find the fay,
Through respiration, drinking in the beams
Of primal Deity, till in the mind
He **sees prefigured the** sweet flower to be :
So **all the** blossoms of the Seasons live.

The universe is made of tiny men :
In holy infancy their endless lives
Round ever to an orb of perfect light :
And matter, in its varying forms and hues
And subtle harmonies of airy flame,
Is their pavilion, where, in choral dance,
They weave the flying tapestry of space.
These are the fays of Nature, brethren small
To Angels and the radiant human kind ;
And love of good and truth, for their own sakes,
And the creative blessedness they bring,
And love of God, who is the Good and True,

His dusky shell her mate forsakes
   In princely robes of green and gold.

The merry elves are in the corn,
   Behold, glad heart, with eyes a-glow;
They dance before the steps of Morn,
   And teach the sprouting wheat to grow.

II.

THE FOUNTAIN OF BEAUTY.

In the Land of Good Affections,
Where the sunlight, where the moonlight,
Are the life-beams of the Father,
Sprang a fountain, and the waters
All were fairies, white and golden.
Worlds on worlds of sportive creatures
In the water-drops were hidden,
And their home was in the fountain,
And their songs were in its laughter.
Worlds on worlds of living beauty,
In each water-drop's gyrations,
Ever rising, never falling,
Circled forth into existence.

G

In the water-drops were nereids,
They were fairies of the waters,
And in merry troops, like rainbows,
Green and golden, red and azure,
They arose in sportive millions,
Beautiful with love and wisdom.

Once a little child lay sleeping,
And the fairies of the fountain
Gathered round him in his slumbers ;
And they crowned him with white blossoms,
With white blossoms without number
From the land of the Immortals :
And the fragrance of the blossoms,
Like a spirit from the waters,
Like fair Undine, ever youthful,
Seem to bend enamored o'er him.

Years on years !—Grown old with sorrows,
No more crowned with childhood's roses,
Lay the aged man a-dying.
He remembered, in departing,
All his life in all its stages,
But the fairest and the sweetest
Of the pictures of remembrance

Was the dream he had in childhood
Of the fairies of the fountain.

Once again in sportive myriads,
Tiny as the motes of Summer,
Dancing in the dying chamber,
Like a rainbow o'er his pillow,
All the fairies of the waters
Grew to clearest sight around him.

Putting forth his hand to grasp them,
As the unweaned babe whose fingers
Clasp the sunbeams from his cradle,
Smiling in his dream to see them
Form themselves in living tableaux,
Lay the old man on his death-bed.

By his side there stood a Poet,
And his eyes in wonder opened
To behold the sight elysian.
"Lo! the aged man is passing,"
Said the stricken group around him,
"'Tis a sign of death, he fancies
That the motes obscure his seeing,
That they darken all the chamber."

But the fairies came with roses
From the Land of Youth and Morning,
From the blessed Land of Angels,
And they wreathed him for his nuptials
With the loved one gone before him.

III.

THE FAIRY'S SUMMER SONG.

I know what Angel tends the rose;
What virtue in the apple grows;
And whence the fragrant summer flowers
Receive their sweet and subtile powers;
And why, when day begins to break,
The joyous birds their song awake:
Through Faith we may an insight win
To Him who dwells the world within.

When fairies blush at lovers' talk;
When cherries redden on the stalk;
When thrushes breed, and robins woo,
And on the eaves the pigeons coo;
When the swift graces of the airs
Make music, fit for bridal pairs;

Through Faith we may the meaning win
Of Him who dwells the world within.

The Earth, in summer-charms arrayed,
Is Wisdom at a masquerade:
Through all a bridal music runs,
From meadow pansies up to suns:
The stars are steadfast in their place
Because they feel the Lord's embrace:
Through Faith we may an insight win
To Christ, who dwells the world within.

IV.

THE FAIRY VISION.

Within my heart I found a grave,
  And, buried there, the Pride of Fame,—
The thought to seek, the wish to crave
  A grand and deathless name.

Upon it, in a little nest,
  And small as human things can be,
Five cooing fairies met my quest:
  I wept the sight to see.

Would that I were again a child
  Like one of these, I prayed within,
So tender, lowly, meek and mild,
  And innocent of sin.

My breathless thought was unexpressed,
  When, in a voice to music wed,
That slid in silence through the breast,
  The five together said,

When Pride of Fame expired, we grew
  To joyous being in its place.''
Afar the fairy-bugles blew :
  Tears trembled on my face.

Oh, God ! I cried, and is it so ?
  When evil loves within us die
Do fairies, pure as virgin snow,
  Their children multiply,

And in us build a green retreat,
  And sing their hymeneal lays,
And, hived within the heart, repeat
  Their litanies of praise ?

The answer on my spirit fell,
  "These are My little ones, who keep
The heart, wherein I come to dwell,
  A pasture for My sheep."

At this, methought, a bleating sound,
  Soft as the laughter of the rain,
Came from the tedded grass around,
  And then He spake again,

" If thou wouldst be an Angel wise,
  Forget thyself, and seek to be
A fairy soul, of infant size,
  In meek humility."

V.

LITTLE BY LITTLE.

Little by little the fairies unfold
Tints in the summer time purple and gold :
Daisy and king cup and hyacinth bold
Little by little are born from the mould :
Little by little the poem is told.

Little by little earth's delicate things
Shape in the darkness the butterfly's wings :

Little by little the queens and the kings
Weave the great lyric that History sings.

Little by little the elf and the fay
Gather the cloud from the spirit away ;
Build in the bosom their bowers of play ;
Build the mind's palace that sparkles with day ;
Build the new heart in the old one's decay.

Little by little the **honey** bee takes
Bread from the flower the south-wind awakes :
Little by little the spirit forsakes
Time when the dawn of eternity breaks :
Little by little **eternity shakes**
From **the white time-cloud** the years that are flakes.
Little **by little the** centuries shed
Snows of forgetfulness over the dead :
Little by little the volume is read
Which the All-Father has traced overhead :
Little by little the soul-wings outspread
Till we are borne where the Seraphim tread.

Beautiful May with her raiment is drest
First where the Angels are sweetest and best ;
Then she goes tripping from east unto west
Sowing her smiles at the Maker's behest ;

Little by little her kisses are prest
On the ripe soul that awakes with the blest.

Little by little the soul that is made
Playmate for Spring in her robe is arrayed,
Mountain and valley and dew-dripping glade,
Where the glad fairies may sport unafraid,
Work in the sunshine or sleep in the shade.

Little by little the fairies, who sip
Life from the kisses that bloom on the lip,
In the rich nectar their goblets may dip,
Ere to their Midsummer revel they trip.

———

Into the dying day ! into the dying day !
I follow the path of the flying fay,
      Into the dying day !

I am no more on earth ! I am no more on earth !
I float in the sphere of a fairy's mirth,
      I am no more on earth !

The vesper flame is lit ! the vesper flame is lit !
I glide away on the soul of it,
      The vesper flame is lit !

Into the sunset star ! into the sunset star !
Where the beautiful dwell in their homes afar,
　　　　Into the sunset star !

Follow the flying breeze ! follow the flying breeze !
That sings from the breath of its melodies,
　　　　Follow the flying breeze !

The south-wind's kisses fail! the south-wind's kisses fail!
The climes of the sunset star unvail,
　　　　The south-wind's kisses fail !

In the dying **day ! into** the dying day !
I follow the path **of the flying fay,**
　　　　Into the dying day !

Part Second.

—

REGINA:

A SONG OF MANY DAYS.

REGINA:

A Song of Many Days.

THE SONG OF REGINA:

I.

WHERE **Æthra's** island, fair and large,
    Rocks like a lotos on the sea,
The Ocean fairies form a barge,—
    A gondola of light for thee.

II.

Their thoughts are in its rapid keel,
    Their pulses urge it on its way:
The waves beneath delight to feel
    Its sheeny winglets o'er them play.

III.

Through antenatal nights and morns,
    A tender mirthful unborn sprite,

Where yon fair crescent shews its horns
   Thou didst respire divine delight.

IV.

Now thou art rising, there to be
   Thy angel-mother's angel-guest,
A dovelet flying from the sea
   In its primeval ark to rest.

V.

When thy young being first began
   'Twas made of hearts and wings and eyes,
And rainbows from the purple span
   Of the Queen Heaven's maternal skies,

VI.

And tender kisses, close and warm,
   From lips of virgins undefiled,
Till, floating through the outward form,
   Thou didst appear on earth a child.

VII.

Retrace thy spirit's pathway back,
   And, bold of heart and swift of wing,
Through memory's pale dissolving wrack,
   Arise from Nature to her King.

VIII.

Beyond the bounds of time and space
    Thy kindred Angels gently call :
Rise to Eternity's embrace ;
    Forsake the part and find the all.

THE VISION OF ENGLAND.

Now through the vaulted centuries
Through walls of iron, through gates of brass,
Through corridors of burnished glass,
And over marble pavements, trod
By ancient sons of Christ the God,
We glided to a golden room,
Where sat a lady at a loom,
Weaving the web of destinies.

Elastic were the threads, and through
Her heart the nervous tendrils ran :
She wove according to the plan
Of God, who through her spirit leant
Above the task whereat she bent :
This was the song meanwhile she sung
In old familiar Saxon tongue,

And the swift words like eagles flew,
And dipped their beaks in burning blood,
From the red heart of all the good,
And afterward, both wise and free,
Flew at her beck and sang to me.

" The vi-kings are old ;
From under Thor's shoulder,
To sea islands bold,
Than sea lions bolder,
They gathered in might :
In the red Danes they came,
In the black ships of night,
Flying ravens of flame.

" Still in Daneland the fair
Hath the Norse-king his throne,
In its mid-winter air
Where the sea-earls make moan,
Upflinging his thought
Underneath the white sails,
Like the sea rainbow caught
From the spouting of whales.

" In naked strength,
At his arm's length,

The giant Daneman draws around
His Danish sphere on English ground."

Out of her heart great Cromwell came
And lightened with his lion eyes,
Then caught the web with **hand of flame**
And cast it through the place of skies,
While like a heaven the **chart unrolled** :
Then thundered he in voice of gold,
" Beyond the dim tempestuous wrack
Flieth the Daneman driven back.
From the Dane-spell set spirit-free,
England shall better thrive by me,
Who am the type of her first force.
England, with her dividing rod,
Shall cleave the seas, bring home the God :
Then mother England be the nurse
Of art, love, plenty, joy and song :
God breaks the bubble of the Wrong."

———

We sped upon our way
And mighty thoughts were booming in my brain
Like battle guns at sea.
The Earth lay **far below,**
Most like some stately **war-ship, that is locked**

H

Yard-arm and yard-arm with a floating hell
Of pirate-demons, who have scourged the waves.
A flag of stars was flying at the fore,
But, streaming redly through the gloom, I saw
High o'er the helm Queen England's double cross :
  There one stood, all **unseen,**
Before the waving of whose steadfast **hand**
The hurtling chain-shot flew with harmless force,
Or, changed to bolts of spirit-lightning, burst,
Hurled backward, spreading death and wild dismay.
This man was Cromwell : in the battle ship
The living force of all heroic hearts
Of Christian men was gathered, and all truths,
Monarchal or Republican, or traced
In dim ancestral charts, or written out
By Freedom's sword-point on the heart of man,
Were perilled in that fierce ensanguined fight.

High o'er the conflict poised in middle air
A Woman and a serpent, and the snake
Had struck its fangs to smite her babe unborn ;
But through her bosom flew a rosy dove
And pierced, with gentle force, the serpent's brain.

  I gazed upon the scene ;
Meanwhile the pages of a living scroll,

Unfolded in my heart of hearts, made plain
That coming day when Truth and Error meet,
And Freedom and Oppression ; when the force
Of God Messiah and the demon strength
Of Crime's red anarch combats for the world.—
    Afar from this we fled
And rested in the peaceful Evening **Star.**

Above the planet there were thrones impearled,
In every throne the image of a world,
And on each throne **an** Angel with a sword
In either hand, but God's eternal Word
Flashed through the blades with lightning never still.
As we drew nigh, each, like a blazing hill
Of amethyst and ruby, met our sight.
Twelve legions of Celestial Spirits, bright
With sevenfold morning, interposed their host
Between our orb and that reposeful coast.
Had earthly or infernal anarch met
One Angel, though a bannered world were set
At his right hand in terrible array,
One glance had melted him and them away,
As painted figures on **a** burning wall.

My heart rose in me with a trumpet call

As I these armies of the Lord espied.
O Earth beware ! within blue heaven abide
Myriads who wait to do God's holy will.
Fill up thy chalice with red murder ! fill !
Declare the Lord but man ; His name deny ;
His Word contemn ; His spirit crucify ;
His children smite ; His inward voice resist ;
Wrap thy grim visage in white fancy's mist,
And think, with sophistries of matter born,
To seal the eyelids of the judgment morn ;
Sell Conscience now as once Iscariot sold
His Master ; say that " Faith is blind and old ;"
A little longer serve at Satan's beck,
Mankind a ruin, and the orb a wreck,
While few remain for Heaven's own sake who dare
Live the great life that all the Angels share,
While few survive to fight the hosts of hell,
Inspired in heart with Love's almighty spell.
Lo ! God has heard ! and hark ! at Nature's gate
The falling doom-strokes now reverberate :
For every tear on earth the Saviour shed
He hath an orb of Angels worldward sped :
For every blood-drop from His brow that fell
He opes a Heaven and overcomes a hell :
His dying words, echoed through all the stars,

Burst from heaven's vault to break all dungeon bars.
Against the impious mighty of the world
Christ from His gospel hath the gauntlet hurled.
Champion of Virtue, clothed in flaming fire,
Before His face all earthly dreams expire:
Inly he calls, makes bare His gleaming blade,
And bids the cruel, in their wrath arrayed,
Who smite the lowly poor, for whom He died,
Behold the face of Jesus crucified.

Aye, God was man! His nature took our own:
He shared our sorrows, bore our sins alone:
High o'er the dreaming world he bends, as one
Watches from Heaven the death-bed of a son.—
But lo! a change. Faith is a waning moon,
'Mid the dead stars lost in a final swoon:
The languid, weary worshippers repose,
And o'er Earth's Iceland hell's red Hecla glows.
Demoniac Visions haunt the midnight air:
Through human eyes the Fallen Angels glare:
From land to land Abaddon blows his blast:
Fierce Pandemonium storms the world at last:
The second advent flames in signs foretold
By every era since the Age of Gold.
Rejoice, ye lovers of the good and true!
Messiah comes! bid every fear adieu.

Messiah comes, **in** still small voices, heard
Deep in the **heart,** like Morn's first herald bird.
Messiah comes, **as to the** unborn child
The travail pain that thrills the mother mild!
Messiah comes! lo! all the skies unroll,
And Nature shudders at the Word's control.
The dust of matter, quivering **to its core,**
Yields to His might and bids mankind adore.
Perdition's death-lamps dwindle where they stand :
In burning row the constellations band
And sing their mighty song of praise to Him.
Hear their sweet litany through ether dim.

GLORIA PATRIA OF THE STARS.

I.

There's not a star on high, that swings
    A censer 'mid the **burning host,**
But in her glory **ever** sings
    To Father, Son and Holy Ghost.

II.

Where sweet Corona's orbéd urn
    Draws rapture from the solar coast,

Her tuneful thoughts in music turn
  To Father, Son and Holy Ghost.

III.

Where Mercury with silver hand
  Unveils her planet's lucid coast,
She lifts her lay in voices grand
  To Father, Son and Holy Ghost.

IV.

The Evening Star upon her throne
  In Christ the Saviour makes her boast,
In Him adoring God alone,
  The Father, Son and Holy Ghost.

V.

The lovely Mars with bridal shame
  Adores her bridegroom Saviour most,
And blushing, owns His mighty name,
  In Father, Son and Holy Ghost.

VI.

In trembling bliss the silver Moon
  Delights to hold an infant host,
Who praise, through life's eternal noon,
  The Father, Son and Holy Ghost.

VII.

Majestic are the tones that fall
    From Jupiter's engirdled coast;
They own Messiah Lord of all,
    In Father, Son and **Holy Ghost.**

VIII.

Where Saturn sweeps with solemn thought,—
    That ancient of the planet host,—
He hath His orb in tribute brought
    To Father, Son and Holy Ghost.

IX.

With tongues of pentecostal flame,
    Apostles of the azure coast,
Messiah God they all proclaim
    In Father, Son and Holy Ghost.

As Dante trod o'er purgatorial coals
    I haunt the sands of Time's drear wilderness,
Wrung with the agonies of ruined souls,
    Death-bound in sin's invincible duress.
I cry aloud until the startled air
    Echoes my hollow voice; and, where I pass,

Destruction threatens me with sabre bare,
.   And Evil Spirits curse: alas! alas!
They mock my sorrows.   Woe, ah, woe is me!
Time smites the dumb lips of Eternity,
And startles at the hollow undertone
Of the great heart that can but inly groan,

The multitudes around my feet are dying
   Like Summer insects, killed by Autumn frost.
The plague of sin upon the soul is lying.—
   Restless on troubled seas mankind are tossed.
While error eats its path with silent curse,
The stars come forth, that living universe,
Arrayed on thrones of unpavilioned light :—
Earth, like a skulking thief, prowls through the night.

I call unto the deep heart of my kind,
   "Awake, for murder haunts thy drowsy head,
And madness darts its venom through the mind,
   And Hades wakes with all its cruel dead,
And rages, in the vices that go forth,
Like hungry locusts, from the fallow earth."

I sow my path with ashes, for the seeds
   Of love I scatter crumble as they fall;
But thick and branchy spread the poisoned weeds,

Whose fruit are crimes the spirit that appal.
Surely the beast hath knowledge; not a bird
But knows its God; yet man rejects the Word.

Wail, ye wild pines ! ye mountain cedars wave
    Your branches to the night winds !   There are cries
From hollow Orcus and the spirit-grave ;—
    A rush of armies through the middle skies ;—
Wail your sad message to the nations dead !
They will not hear until the skies are red
With the war-eagles, who have come to feast
On dainty flesh of human kind and beast ;
While the white fire-wolves, leaping from the cloud
Of retribution, fasten on the proud.

THE CHANT OF JUDGMENT.

Solemnly as death-bells toll
At the passage of a Soul,
While its deeds, a flying scroll,
Vast and wondrously unroll
Vistas to the burning goal ;
        Toll, toll, toll,
            Toll for the dead !

From the World's deep heart a knell,
With reverberating **swell,**
Through my silent spirit fell,
Speeding far to Heaven and **hell** :
Tongued with judgment was the bell :
    Toll, toll, toll,
        Toll for the dead !

Heart within me, like a bird
By the harps of Morning stirred,
Thou didst echo to the Word
By the first-born Angels heard :
    Toll, toll, toll,
        Toll for the dead !

Heart, my heart, astonished **then**
Thou didst view the souls of men,
Some like tigers from their den,
Some **too** pure for mortal ken,
Breathe the breath of judgment, when
Time, departing, cried " Amen !
    Toll, toll, toll,
        Toll for the dead !"

Crownless anarchs, fierce and bold,
Who for pride or lust or gold

Had their brethren slain or sold,—
Over them the doom bell tolled,
Ere the breathing fire-wave rolled,
Prophesied by Scriptures old,
      " Toll, toll, toll,

   Toll for the dead !"

Fraud and pretence fled away ;
Fashion doffed her rich array ;
Wanton souls, all madly gay,
Felt the pulse of riot stay,—
Heard the Judgment Angel say
   " Toll, toll, toll,

      Toll for the dead !"

The hoar-frost on the threshold of the **world**
Melts to a golden mist before the sun :
The Judgment Angel hath his page unfurled ;
A thousand centuries expire in one.
A typhoon strikes the rapid bark of Time ;
With purple sails, in pennons torn and flying,
She slowly sinks, **to** ocean's oozy slime :
Grim tyrants **inly** feel their empires dying.
Like the she **Borgia's** victims at their feast,
Delirious men drink poison in their wine,
Expiring turn their faces from the east,

Then wake, deformed to serpents, wolves and swine,
With human voice changed to a demon cry,
Spurned from the loathing earth, abandoning the sky.

Mark ye that mighty City by the sea,
Which drains the Old World's heart to feed the New:
Chameleon-like, it takes its livery
From every blazoned vice that flaunts to view.
The greed of gold has left its yellow stain
Upon the jaundiced face, the taloned hand;
The aspic, envy, and the blind worm, pain,
Hive in its heart, like adders in the sand:
The swarming larvæ of corruption feed
Upon the body of the Commonweal;
A thousand wounds, that fester while they bleed,
And taint the reeking air, its foul disease reveal.

This is the young Republic's pride and boast,
The type and microcosm of mankind.
Art, Arms, Trade, Fashion, lead the stormy host
New sins to fathom, new disease to find.
Hang out the Lazaretto's yellow flags,
Death haunts the crowded street, the gay saloon.
Crime whets the knife and hides it in his rags;
And Misery mutters " Night is coming soon."

Boyhood anticipates the sins of man;
Precocious childhood drains the draught of hell;
They build their lives while Satan schemes the plan,
And, in their boastful breasts, infernal anarchs dwell.

To lie, to game, to cozen and to curse,
To rob the neighbor, with defiant brow
And lecherous lip to pass from bad to worse,
Debars no man from place and glory now.
Gorged Infamy in self-complacence dies,
While Conscience vainly pleads within the breast :
The ledger of the soul is filled with lies :
Sin lulls them to a deep and drowsy rest :
The lamps of Faith in pallid smoke expire :
They smite God's Holy Word, and say, " Be dumb!"
But, hark ! the thunders of the judgment-choir!
The books are opened now, the trial day is come.

As Jonah stood in Nineveh of old
I wake, emerging from the selfhood's tomb.
High on a throne of firmamental gold,
Shines the MESSIAH,—breaks the day of doom.
The souls of men within their bodies turn,
Like the unresting dead within their graves;
Deep in their breasts the vengeful furies burn ;

They quench their thirst in passion's fiery waves;
They call upon the mountains and the rocks
Of outward thought, care, fancy, fame and pride
To hide them from the Saviour; each one mocks
The foot-fall of the doom whose coming few shall bide.

The graves are opened; from their sepulchre
Mercy and Peace and Justice reappear;
And holy hearts and consciences, astir
With inward faith and love and hope draw near;
A new Apocalypse of flamy walls,
And jasper battlements, and streets of gold,
And gates of pearl, and angel-pictured halls,
The Lord's redeemed in spirit now behold:
And, "Come, ye blessed of the Father," cries
The inward Saviour, "enter into rest;
I have prepared this beauteous paradise
For all who have My name in heart and life confest."

Hark, there are voices in the air,
    When pitying Love the poor relieves,
Sweet, to the bleeding heart of care,
    As music that the south wind weaves.
And, where the lowly kneel by night,
    And rise in peace, with sins forgiven,

All radiant with seraphic light,
   They pass through slumber's door to Heaven.

And there are Angels, pure and wise,
   With hearts like doves upon the wing,
Where Grief consumes the night **with sighs,**
   And Anguish feels the serpent-sting.
Soft through the air the blessing steals,
   Till slumber balms the aching eyes;—
A noble life its dawn reveals,
   The poor awake in Paradise.

Forget the grief, the wrong forgive,
   For they who bear misfortune's load
In patient love, alternate live
   On earth with care, in sleep with God!
Day hath its woes, its transient pains,
   But slumber soothes the weary breast,
Then, where the Lord of Mercy reigns,
   We enter, in His love to rest.

Life's bitter cup may brim with tears,
   But, when we drink in faith divine,
" He who hath loved us" oft appears,
   And turns the briny wave to wine.

And half our life is dark and drear,
  Where Sorrow's north wind rudely blows ·
And half in God Messiah's sphere,
  Tranced like the dew-drop in the rose.

Lift up! lift up! ye heavenly gates,
  That all who love may enter in!
A second day-spring there awaits
  The eyes that wept for mortal sin;
Till sleep and waking grow complete,
  When **Day and Night** their Saviour see,
And Earth and Heaven rejoice to meet,
  And sound the Year of Jubilee!

A Spectre rose, in whom **ten thousand deaths**
Concentred in one dying; **livid fear**
Breathed in the hoar-frost of his chilly breath,
And palsied with its touch the atmosphere.
Couched in his breast a venomed serpent spat
Its curse upon the living, and they grew
Enamored of all evil things thereat,
And loathed the holy, and abhorred the true.
From heart to heart the rank infection spread,
And, coiling in the mighty serpent's train,

I

They **drank his** blood, and ate his flesh for bread,
Till the huge viper lived enthroned in every brain.

Like death-drops, in one poison cup, the ghost
Held them till in the ferment of their **lust ;**
Then drank the spirit of their maniac host,
And so possessed them to the very dust.
They walk the streets ; their pampered passions **crave**
All wealth, dominion, splendor, pride and place :
Their spirits fester rankly in the grave ;
Within their hearts ten thousand deaths embrace.
These are the petty tyrants of their kind :
Self-love **the god** whom each in heart adores :
To faith, love, pity, **cold** and **deaf and blind**
They sit, in secret lodge, while **demons tile the doors.**

Their name is Legion : ye may know them well !—
Self-love the sole religion which they preach.
None trusts his neighbor ; each for gold will sell
That holy place wherein the Angels teach.
Masked **in** a garb of falsehood and pretence
They plead, write, act, as Interest leads the way,
Till **brutal instinct grows** their only sense :
Fixed **in** their guilt they wait the judgment day :
Like the dead sun wrapt in a disk of fire,

Pouring dense midnight from its lurid urn,
They inundate the world with evils dire:
They bolt the gates of mind that Christ may not return.

"There is no God but Self alone,"
    Their spirits inly cry,
"And he who sits on Mammon's throne
    Is Lord and King most high.

"No man but hath his market price,—
    No woman's heart or hand.
Gold holds the keys of Paradise,
    And none his guile withstand.

"'Tis gold that builds the stately house,
    And turns the minstrel's rhymes.
'Tis gold that wins the sweetest spouse,
    Though bought by countless crimes.

"He who to serve the neighbor holds,
    Becomes a dupe and thrall;
And Heaven, beyond the world, unfolds,
    If Heaven there be, for all."

The coldness of the sepulchre exhales
From honeyed lips: the rankness of the dead

Pollutes the living : through the spicy gales
Float larvæ on the world's putrescence fed.
The taint of rotting bodies robs **the** dust
Of elemental virtue.   **Through the air**
A slow destructive poison, born of lust
And hate and pride **and envy, walks with bare**
And silent feet.   The Spirits of Disease
Flit with the boding winds, and, when they spy
Pale earthlings at their revels, unto these
They whisper, and the flesh knows that its doom is nigh.

Mothers their infants murder yet unborn ;
Half clad **the tender, wailing spirits grieve :**
Like crysales, impaled upon **a thorn,**
Their ante-natal **torture** they receive.
O earth is cruel when the mother kills
Her own enwombéd children : white as snow
Its little life each unknown martyr spills :
But their dissolving bodies eat, **with slow**
Consuming fevers, through the nerves, and turn
To fiery scorpions, and infect the breast.
Blue corpse-lights o'er the bridal banquet burn,
And in the marriage cups the grapes of hell are press'd.

The Maniac Soul laughs, in its drunken glee,

While sweet Perdition folds it, and it borrows
From midnight's gay and guilty revelry,
An opiate to lull to sleep its sorrows.
With painted cheeks of artificial bloom
To-day their beauties they adorn and cherish:
To-morrow comes, and, in the jaws of doom,
They pine, they pale, they wither and they perish.
What fruit shall ripen from a seed so base?
They reap as they have sown: unholy still
They flaunt like harlots in the nether space,
Or struggle up to earth as temptresses to ill.

A gay and gilded steamer leaves to-night.
Room for the man of millions at the feast!
Who is this maiden, robed in dainty white,
. Bought by the gold of that luxurious beast?
Upon her finger shines the marriage ring.
Soul! why so mutely in thy temple bleeding?
Despair above sweeps down with raven wing.—
Swiftly we haste the silent stars out-speeding.
Hear ye that plunge? The white-robed one is gone.
O God! she sinks beneath the sullen waters.
Heard ye the death-wail of the plumy swan?
What frenzy wrapt away that fair one of the daughters?

Hadst thou no pity, Man? The guilt be thine,

Be her's forgiveness.   Better thus to be,
A maniac, weltering in the sullen brine.
God's Angels walk in glory on the sea!
Thy gold will buy another.   Let her rest :
But, when thou art upon thy dying pillow,
Beside thee shall be found a Phantom Guest,
In dripping robes emerging from the billow.
"Thou didst not slay her," sayst thou?   Said not Cain
Unto the Lord, "Am I my brother's keeper?"
Thou human tiger! gnash thy teeth in vain :
'Twas thine to sow the tares, but Heaven shall send the
        reaper.

Eternity to-day is but a cloud
Upon the far horizon, white and small;
But yet the gay, the cruel and the proud,
Wrapt in its fury, shall be spectres all.
A war horse, trampling down despairing souls,
To-day thou art, O worldling! but apace
Comes Death, the rider!   Where perdition rolls,
Through blazing tempests, he may urge thy race.
Sin ripens fast in Christendom ; the years
Fold their swift pinions at Messiah's feet ;
And eighteen centuries of human tears
Burst, through the shivered sky, in steams of judgment heat.

Come in, thou Christ! Thou great Unbidden, come!
Sit with us; we have built a house of prayer,
With blazoned Angels pictured walls and dome,
And writ Thy Name amid the glories there.
Guido hath drawn the mild Madonna's face;
Correggio hung Thine image on the cross;
And Raffaelle mirrored forth each act of grace,
Whereby Thou didst retrieve us from the loss.
The sacred song from reverent thousands flows;
Attendant priests perfume the holy aisle,
And awful morning, 'like a judgment rose,'
Blushes through crimson glass to light the mystic pile.

Come in, thou Christ! Like weeping Magdalen,
Behold Thy people, who their sins deplore.
Mount the high pulpit, mild and meek as when
Thou didst for Zion's blindness weep of yore.
Jesus have pity on us. We have gone
In this vile Mammon-worship far astray:
We have no cross to nail our sins upon:
Our lips confess Thee, but our lives betray.
We build thee temples, but deny Thee bread:
Hate rules the heart, and frenzy fires the brain:
Thou hast within no place to lay thine head:
The very Pagans cry, "The Christian's God is gain."

We dare not act our vileness, lest at last
Thou shalt in Heaven deny us; but we dare
Not act Thy precepts wholly, lest the blast
Of scandal shall us lunatics **declare.**
We palter with convictions; we uphold
In act the cruel deeds that demons love.
Wolves tear the very lambs in Zion's fold,
And the gorged adder feeds upon the dove.
Vice thrives in all our cities; babes are sold
By manhood to perdition, and, at night,
Thy image is betrayed for lust or gold,
And yet we dare not hurl the thunderbolts of Right.

We list to little sermons, glibly **spoken;**
We give our little alms, with little thought
How many hearts at every breath are broken,
How many murders of the spirit wrought.
Beneath the splendid chandeliers of Sin
We keep gay time to music on the floors,
While trampled Virtue, like a spectre thin,
Starves in her cot, or freezes at the doors.
To outward seeming we our days conform,
Till seeming seems **a** virtue, when we might
Sound to the blast the trumpet of Reform,
And wake the sleeping world with flames of morning light.

Earth is a madhouse. Sin and sanity
Live not within one dwelling: none are wise
Till the Lord Christ through inward faith they see;
Till selfish lust within the bosom dies.
Men build the house before they occupy:
The fiends, who haunt the palaces of hell,
Reared them before they died: Eternity
Glooms round us long before the burial-knell.
Space is projected spirit: after death
The murderer's thoughts are daggers in his hand;
Flames kindle from the hot magnetic breath,
And, in their furnace-heat, the lost in Tophet stand.

All is objective there that bad men hide
On earth in secret caverns of deceit.
Infatuate Spirits, in their loathsome pride,
As warring gods in hostile squadrons meet.
The sinner is the devil's telescope,
Through whom this outward world the fiend espies.
Foul consciences are plains with downward slope,
That disappear where lost Gomorrah lies.
Earth's atoms to a common centre fly;
Base passions link the base, their hearts are one;
One world is theirs, and in its graves lie,
Stung by the snaky beams of its infernal sun.

When bad men pass beyond the gates of sleep
Like obscene wolves they herd in bands together :
Infernal anarchs, from their fiery **deep,**
Nerve them to deeds which shall mankind dissever.
There fertile Fancy schemes **to-morrow's** wrongs ;
Hate plots its murders ; Lust its crafty wiles :
Perdition's poet there conceives his songs,
And sleek Hypocrisy invents its guiles :
In gloomy synods priestly bigots plan
New sorceries of doctrine for the mind :
There tyrants scheme the slavery of man,
And forge the darts that kill, and link the chains that
    bind.

Oh ! there are tyrants, fierce and strong,
  On earth by day, in hell by night ;
They sleep to plot with Satan's throng :
  They wake to slay with morning light.

And there are priests of high degree,
  Who seek the dark, infernal doors,
And in their slumbers turn the key
  That opes Gehenna's burning floors.

And there are Angels, wise and vast,
  Who brand them on the face and hand :

These are the Witnesses, at last,
　　Accusing from the Judgment Land.

———

Heaven fills its nurseries from married minds,
And hearts in nuptial virtue that rejoice:
Hell the adulterer to its thraldom binds,
Lurks in his glance and ruins in his voice.
The Wanton seeks her guilty paramour
In spirit, and, beyond the world's dim portals,
Their sorceries they meditate before
The gloomy synods of the lost Immortals.
The gay coquette who airs her painted charms
In Fashion's madness, pleased that slaves adore her,
Is whirled within some viewless Python's arms,
With masked and subtle fiends insatiate bending o'er her.

Fold to thy heart that fair one, whom the Lord
Hath, as thy bosom friend and consort, given:
Within her breast conjugial joys are stored;
O'er her calm pillow float the doves of Heaven.
Love her in God: His peace, through her descending,
Shall soothe thee from the cares of earth afar,
And thou shalt wake, through sleep, to love unending,
Tranced in some beauteous hymeneal star;

There, crowned with sweetness, she will smile to meet
    thee,—
Through inmost love the Inmost Heaven is won,—
There the fraternal Angels throng to greet thee,
And God Messiah beam, throned in the Marriage Sun.

Oh ! there are nuptial joys, **that flow**
    Through sinless realms of inward rest :
The bridal roses freshly blow,
    The love-birds carol in the breast :

There, o'er the bridegroom's dreamy tent,
    And o'er the **young bride's** blissful eyes,
Messiah's threefold Heaven **is bent,**
    And shine the **lamps of Paradise.**

And there are Angels, blithe and fair,
    Who crown their silent rest, by **night,**
With flowers that bloom in Eden air
    From inward thoughts of **heart-delight :** .

And where the two in one agree
    To live the life their Lord inspires,
Through sleep **they** rise in Heaven to be,
    And worship with Messiah's choirs.

I have seen another city:
How in words shall I describe it?
Language fails before the splendor,
As the sight of the disciples
Was obscured upon Mount Tabor,
When their Lord shone forth transfigured.

Eighteen hundred years that city
Grew in circles from its centre.
Massive gold were its foundations:
All its gates of pearl were fashioned:
All the wealth of all the nations
Found a place amidst its treasures:
Gems on gems, a countless number,
As the spirit stars for glory,
In its massive walls were gathered.
Spire and minaret and column,
Nave and frieze and arch and buttress,
All were built of stones most precious.

Through the streets there ran a river,
And the waves in their vibrations
Sang with infinite rejoicings;
And the blind, who bathed within them,
Saw, with vision never darkened:

And the deaf, who bathed within them,
Heard the music of the Angels :
And the sick, who bathed within them,
Were restored to health and vigor :
And the old, who bathed within **them,**
Felt the mask of age dissolving,
Felt the youthful bloom returning.
And the dying bathed within them,
And the Angel Death, beside them,
Gently bowed, and smiled and vanished,
For their life became immortal.

O the wonders of the City !
Where the fruit-trees dropt their leafage
It was wafted east and westward
For the healing of the nations.
There the tribes of God were gathered :
There the slave forgot his bondage :
There the poor forgot his hunger :
There the sad forgot his sorrows :
Tears were wiped from all their faces,
And their mournful days were ended.
There they had no need of sunlight,
Nor the pale moon's tender crescent,
Nor the gentle stars **to** light them.

All who dwelt there were transfigured
By the light of God within them:
And the temple cast no shadow,
For the gem-like walls were burning
With a light of inward glory.

No man questioned of his brother
If he knew the Mighty Builder,
For His mystic name was written
On their palms and breasts and foreheads,
And His light was on their faces,
And His gladness in their spirits.
Some were wiser than the others,
But they gained their truth in loving;
'Twas the heart that knew within them.
Some were richer than the others,
But their treasures grew by giving,
And their ceaseless benefactions,
Like the flood-tides of the ocean,
Filled their bosoms in returning.
Some were stronger than the others,
But they labored most in silence,
And their very rest was action,
And their very stillness music,
And their very touch was healing,

For the selfhood was forgotten,
And the being merged in uses.

When they worshipped all responded,
In an hymeneal chorus,
For their hearts, as one, were wedded,
And the Bridegroom dwelt within them.
But their worship had no sameness :
Some, in silent, secret trances,
Knelt and prayed like Saint Theresa,
When she floated in devotion
O'er the gratings of the convent :
Some, like stout old Martin Luther,
Sang the mighty German music,—
Thundered loudly the old hundred :
Some, like meek and good A Kempis,
Slowly paced through nave and chancel,
While the heart within the bosom
Pealed an organ-like Te Deum :
Some, like Cromwell and his soldiers,
Worshipped to the sound of trumpets,
Keeping time with sword and buckler.

Some adored at early morning
With the sunlight on their faces ;

Some at sunset, when the blossoms
Breathe their fragrant prayers to heaven:
All were true to their vocation.
Helping hands to lift the lowly
Each possessed, they were his birthright;—
Faith and hope and martyr courage,
Love, beyond the bounds of Nature,
Lasting as eternal ages.

Eighteen hundred years have vanished.—
Time his judgment bell is pealing
With an awful Dies Iræ.
Eighteen hundred years have vanished,
And the cross of Christ, ascending,
Triumphs o'er the constellations,
Shining there in light eternal.
But the city still grows brighter;
All its gates of pearl are opened;
All its waters pour their healing;
All its fruit-trees yield their ripeness;
And the earth awakes at midnight,
On her dying pillow turning,
To behold the wondrous vision.
There the good of all the ages
Bid the earthly brother welcome.

K

Wouldst thou know this mighty city?
'Tis the Church our Saviour founded.
All the good are His disciples;
All the loving are His servants;
All the pure in heart His children;
They are one through all the ages.
Names and creeds that breed dissension
Are but shadows of the Earth-world;
All are one in Christ their Saviour.

Creeds and names and forms and systems
Here have bound the loving-hearted;
But the sect-wall slowly moulders,
Christ is calling to His children,
" Come and worship me in freedom;
In the loving heart's dilation;
In the inner soul's expansion;
In the inner Word's unfolding.
Let the names of party perish."

They shall find the Holy City,
With their spirit-senses opened,
Who obey the Voice within them :
They shall walk in shining raiment
Where the temples cast no shadow.

All the past revives its glory.
As the old man slowly dieth
To become a spotless Angel,
So, in agonies of Nations,
Cleaving outward forms asunder,
Shines the Christendom of ages,
Putting on its snow-white garments,
Robed with light and love immortal.

———

Oh! the blessed fairy voices!
In this tranquil summer twilight,
By the gentle flowing river,
They are singing on within me;
" Rise and listen, thou beloved!
Leave the Earth-world to its shadow;
Turn thee to the Land of Morning."

Sweet are ye, O fairy brothers,
Children of returning Eden.
Thrilled in spirit by the summons
I am lifted and translated:
Mortal sorrows are forgotten:
I am welcomed in a temple
Where the walls are truths eternal
From the Holy Word I treasure.

K 2

City of the Lyric Angels!
Palace of the Choral Muses!
Here, on thrones of light enkindled,
Sit the poets of the nations.
All the atmosphere **is vocal**:
They are chanting of the wonder ;
Man returning to the newness ;
Man the breath of God respiring,
Drinking in the Love and Wisdom
Of the Infinite All-Father ;
From the love of self delivered ;
Consciously at one with Nature ;
Moving in the spheral motion
Of the planetary systems ;
Bathing in the boundless rapture,
Chanting in the varied numbers
Of the Spirits and the Angels ;
Building from the fluent music
Of the Word of God unfolding ;
Weaving life into an epic
In the grand heroic measure,
While the World Soul thrills to hear it,
And the planets wake the echo.

Twofold, and consciously at one
With the glad seasons and the triad year,
     I dwell in Earth and Heaven.
'Tis sweet to muse amid these ruins gray,
And watch the white moon o'er the twilight sea
Float in her silver barge, resting reclined
     Beneath this holy fane:
But sweeter far, through spiritual sense,
With Regina the beautiful and pure,
To climb the hills of Morning Land, and gaze
Upon the varied scenes of many worlds,
     With kindling heart aglow,
And, from the warp and woof of Heaven and Earth,
To weave the tapestry of song divine,
     Where mortal poets fail.

LAYS OF BOLTON ABBEY.

I.

THE RUINS.

WITHIN the gray monastic pile
The annual daisies bloom and smile,

While o'er the roofless cloister shine
Heaven's altar lamps with light divine.

Where holy men their **ave** said,
The Angels pace **with** stately **tread**;
And deeds of mercy, **all** forgot,
Devote to Heaven the hallowed spot.

Not vain the Faith, that dwelt apart
And sought its God with chastened heart :
The self-renouncing mind and will
Could hold divine communion still.

What though, within their darkened age,
They saw but **dim** the sacred page?
Truth from her Scripture drew **for them**
The crucifix and diadem.

The vestures of their age decay ;
Their time-worn temples pass away ;
But still the Church eternal stands,
A shrine not built by human hands.

Steadfast in glory as in shame
Burns on the one immortal flame ;

O'er mossy stones of fallen creeds
Bloom the sweet flowers of kindly deeds;

And through the roofless arches beam,
From depths of light and love serene,
The splendors of that threefold ray,
The Word, that fills all Heaven with day.

II.

THE PROTESTANT REFORM.

Why fell the Faith men call "the old"
In ivied ruins dark with mould?
Because it failed the Word to scan,
For lack of sympathy with man.

In vain the vast cathedral pile,
Where pictured saint and angel smile,
If, in the splendors of the spot,
The end of worship is forgot.

That end the Inward Christ makes plain;
'Tis love and light in heart and brain;
The freedom of the soul from all
The sceptic's doubt, the bigot's thrall.

Vain are the creeds, that seek to bind,
When God would liberate the mind;
For still the Word leads on the race
To God Messiah's vast embrace.

III.

APOSTOLIC SUCCESSION.

To every age **the** Lord of Light
Sends forth Apostles **of the** Right:
The living voice, the burning pen
Interpret still **His Word to** men.

When Faith is weak and **Love is cold,**
Oppression fierce and Sorrow bold,
And the dead herbage of the past
Chokes down the springing germs **at last,**

Some fervent soul, from sense **apart,**
Grows vocal at Messiah's heart,
With pen or sword arm smites the keys,
And wakens Earth with harmonies.

Then sudden **growths of** fruit and flowers
Attest the world's reviving powers,
And, through the shivered bolts and bars,
Men walk in freedom like the stars.

IV.

THE MARTYRS.

Oh! ye, who **wear the** sackcloth of affliction,
    Be patient and be calm:
Peace, the **great** Angel, breathes her benediction,
    From lips distilling **balm.**

Be resolute, against all foes prevailing:
    Keep the soul's image bright
And beautiful, **for the sublime** unveiling
    Beyond this transient night.

On you shall rest the fiery tongues and cloven
    Descending from the **Word**;
And **fall** white robes, in Heaven's effulgence woven,
    Beloved of the Lord!

V.

THE SECRET OF POESY.

The soul who Christ in **Nature sees**
May touch the great **world's organ** keys,
And wake the high and **awful base**
That thunders through the **suns of space.**

O **Master of the** Lyric Band
Who sweep the chords of Morning Land,
Creation stands, cathedral-wise,
A temple whence Thy praises rise.

The rounded songs that shape the star
Borne from Thy Spirit's fulness are,
And Earth repeats the strain again
Through octaves of angelic men.

The thoughts, that leave Thy radiant **face,**
Bloom in the pictured fields of space :
Those glorious visions all inroll
To shape the landscapes of the soul.

As where resistless oceans dwell,
Set in the dim world's hollow shell,

So deep, so vast, within the span
Of heart and mind Thou art with man.

Joy, beauty, valor, worth and love,
The types below of Heaven above,
That touch the soul on every chord,
Are breathings of Thy essence, Lord!

VI.

A MEDITATION OF PURITY.

Blest are the Pure in Heart, who press
The saintly lips of Righteousness,
And win their chaste angelic grace
Where Truth and Charity embrace.

Through purity the Lord is found,
And Eden springs on earthly ground,
While the great Scriptures all unfold
Their flowers and fruits of starry gold.

Through purity the heart receives
The nuptial crown the Angel weaves,
While in the bosom flow the heats
Out-born from Heaven's conjugial sweets.

Through purity the breast respires
From God Messiah's breathing fires,
While Heaven's descending raptures bloom
Immortal o'er the selfhood's **tomb.**

Through purity **Heaven's joys infill**
The senses with their **tender thrill;**
The **fay** within the heart is shrined ;
The Muses grace the vocal mind.

Through purity the constant breast
Inhales the paradisal rest,
And the wrapt soul communing hears
The silver music of the Spheres.

VII.

THE MISTLETOE.

The Druid, from the aged oak,
To grace his fearful penance, broke
  With murmured prayers and low,
The plant belovéd by the **dead ;**
And Odin's awful rites were said
  Beneath the mistletoe.

Thank God! a better day succeeds,
And, from the dim ancestral creeds,
　To clearer light we rise.
Star of the East, thou shinest now
On Christian England's queenly brow,
　Anointed from the skies.

When Christmas-day returns again,
With festive cheer for peaceful men,
　And charity for all,
The mistletoe shall still be found,
From the pale winter's brow unbound,
　To grace the festival.

With something of a kindly beam,
Through its dim leaves the Past shall gleam,
　While, with divinest light,
The Star of God Messiah's love
Irradiates the land above,
　And gilds the Christmas night.

VIII.

A MEDITATION OF MEEKNESS.

Blest are the meek, for they shall reign
　As kings by grace divine,

When floral wreaths are all the chain
　　That peaceful nations twine ;
When, heart to heart, and hand to hand,
　　The peoples all unite ;
And Freedom **rears her palace** grand,
　　On Order's kingly height.

For wisest minds in meekness grow
　　To sceptre and to crown,
Nor can their royal state foreknow
　　Until the Lord comes down.
They climb **the** bright imperial stairs
　　Of use to all the free,
And sit, enthroned, amid **the prayers**
　　Of glad Humanity.

IX.

ENGLAND'S NEW ERA.

Who shall **behold the** glorious day
　　When, on **Britannia's** brow,
Shall flame the pentecostal ray,
　　Her Heaven that brightens now?

When stream **the** splendors of the Word,
   Her sons with peace to bless,
And through her radiant mind is poured
   The Light of Righteousness?

Celestial in its beauty then
   Her Holy Church **must be,**
Where myriads of rejoicing men
   Adore in unity;
Where all shall inly know the Lord
   Of truth and love divine;
And bloom anew great Aaron's **rod**
   To grace her priestly trine.

How sweet shall be her sacred songs
   When multitudes adore,
And Heaven with all angelic tongues
   Replies for evermore:
When hearts below and hearts above
   At one divinely thrill,
And God Messiah's perfect love
   Inspires the common will!

X.

ASCENSION OF THE YEAR.

The ripened fruits, to earth that fall,
And grace the Autumn's festive hall,
  Or crown her banquet **now,**
Were buds bedewed by **April showers,**
Or hung displayed, in airy flowers,
  Upon the teeming bough.

Though by a thousand perils crost,
The Year's first promise was not lost,
  And, while she hastes away,
Through all the mild maternal skies,
The nobler Seasons yet to rise
  Before her vision play.

From God Messiah's face **she came,**
Veiled in the sun's transparent flame,
  And, through the planet's mould,
In constant light and heat, she poured
The truth and goodness of the Lord,
  And bade its germs unfold.

Form of His bounty, large and **free,**
With gifts for all Humanity,

From Heaven to Earth she trod :
Great Year ascend, and offer up
Our heart's libations in thy cup,—
  Our gratitude to God !

———

What Spirit Huntress blows her horn?
  'Tis Dian, mistress of the night.
No more on weary Earth forlorn,
  She calls me to her house of light.

Here let me muse of stately themes,
  With Poets in her lyric hall.
The Spirit Sun upon me beams ;
  I chant the pre-Adamic fall,

And, rising, float in airy space,
  Through visioned empires far and wide,
While, mild of heart, and fair of face,
  My sister Angel moves beside.

———

Great Dian blows her silver horn :
  The dying echoes fail afar ;
For we behold that ampler morn
  Whence all her lucid glories are.

L

Upon the threshold of the day
  We pause, the Minstrel's goal is won.
Well have ye borne us on our way,   *Regina*
  Ye wingéd horses of the sun.

LUTEIA: THE MARTYR POET OF THE STAR THAT FELL.

PRELUDE.

GENIUS of Nature! thou celestial Muse,
Who art coeval with thy brother Time
  And thy sweet sister Space;
Who dost possess for thy great memory
  The universal past,
And sun thyself in all-creative light;
While God inspires thee, rise from all thy stars;
Gather the ripe years for my chalice now,
And press the thoughts of thy most ancient race
In golden grapes that I may drink the wine.
Genius of Nature! draw thine Isis veil;
Flash through my soul the splendors of thy face;
Enfold me to thy heart and thrill me there
With the quick pulses of Eternal Love;

So shall I sing from no fantastic spell,
Rehearse no fiction, born from the embrace
Of the wild reason and self-loving will,
But tune my lyre to oracles divine.

THE JOURNEY.

We sat one day, my friend and I, conversing
    Of perished empires populous and old,
Till the great Sun, that mighty past rehearsing,
    Pictured our thought in heaven's aërial gold,
Then disappeared in evanescent glory.
"So ends," my brother cried, "Earth's visionary story."

But look! the stars come out in stately choirs!
    My spirit answered that complaining voice:
"Ah!" he responded, "they are funeral pyres
    Perchance: none ever heard the stars rejoice:
'Tis a sad sight, a grave-yard without end:"
His heart held secret tears: thereat I left my friend.

I was a poor man, born to many ills:
    Alone I fought a veiled mysterious fate:

L 2

I braced my feet against the rugged hills
   And journeyed on, while more and more the weight
Of the world's anguish, and the common lot,
Ensepulchred my heart, that its own woes forgot.

I sank to sleep beneath an aged palm ;
   A little fountain bubbled at its root ;
A Stranger came, with oil and wine and balm,
   And nourished me with strange delicious fruit ;
Then, when the night grew drowsy, " Come and rest,"
He said, "thy aching head awhile upon My breast."

I knew Messiah ! awed, yet flying not.
   A second life within my veins began :
He led me to a wild sequestered grot,
   In mountain solitudes unknown by man.
He touched my lids, and scales fell from mine eyes,
Then inwardly I woke with Him in Paradise.

He called me sister, brother, spouse and friend,
   And, while in love and wonder I adored,
Transported me to realms of light unkenned,
   Where orbs of angels own Him God and Lord,
And Friend and Father : while they gathered round,
" Rejoice with Me," He cried, " one that was lost is found."

Here with that goodly company I dwell,
   And tears are wiped away from all our eyes;
He is our rock, our shade, our cooling well,
   Heart's joy, soul's peace, hope's anchor, light of skies:
His breast our pasture, we the sheep he loves;
His very heart our home, and we Messiah's doves.

One came to me, in that delicious home,
   Whom I had loved on earth a little while.
It was my mother. "Look!" she cried, "the dome
   Of Heaven is filled with day; Messiah's smile
Unfolds the heart as morning opes the rose.
In choral hymns we wake to worship from repose.

      "Only as the Lord inspires
      Angel-poets tune their lyres:
      Only as the selfhood dies
      Life unfolds its melodies:
      Kissed by lips of Love Divine
      We may taste the lyric wine.

      "Look! the crimson stars appear,
      Floating in the crystal mere
      Of the spangled skies, the Night
      Blushes from her Maker's sight:

Lift the heart and bend the knee :
Hark the morning jubilee !

" See that star of portent grand
Over Aldebaran's land ;
'Tis thy birth-star, thou wert born
Underneath its mellow morn,
And the long Saturnian line
In its music hail the Nine.

" 'Tis the Poet's orb, the one
Nearest to the Lyric Sun :
But a fairer sphere behold,
Once Canopus called of old,
'Tis the star of trances deep
Ruling well the Poet's sleep.

" Lo ! another, eastern yet,
Bright with jewelled coronet ;
That the star of stars for thee,
Wisest of the lyric three,
For thy ante-natal flame
From its lamp of ruby came.

" Chanting with a sweet refrain,
Riding steed without a stain,

From a realm of purest mould,
Steeped in Morn's most perfect gold,
Never yet by earthling seen
Hastes the fair Luteian queen. *Regina*

" As the mist-wreath leaves the rills,
As the sunlight mounts the hills,
Or the pearl dissolves in wine,
Cease from Nature's annual vine;
Rise to Heaven's embracing air;
Thrill to joy and music there.

" Here sit with me, while still Perfection draws
    Thy spirit from its past, whose memory
Forgets itself in joy, and learn the laws
    Which are creation's order : Look, and see,
And tell me then thy visions."   I replied,
Mother, my heart cleaves to thy tender side.

But lo! a chariot, drawn by doves, descending.
    Twelve eagles compass it as with a ring;
Their white wings thrill the air with bliss unending,
    And in it beams, apparelled as a king,
A prince from Jupiter; my soul to him
Leaps thrillingly, I call him Zapthalim.

His frame is cast in Nature's noblest mould :
   Thereat she smiled and said, "I leave you now,
He will those mighty mysteries unfold,
   Which are the gifts of Poets, who endow
Life's common speech with wonders not its own."
She spake and vanished.   I was not alone ;

For in her place a tender maiden stood ;
   Her eyes were like two heavens of clearest weather,
That, full of starlight, gaze into the flood,
   Till sky and ocean seem to thrill together.
She bore a rod with milk-white myrtles bound ;
Her brows with hyacinth and rose were crowned.

We were twin buds of one maternal stem ;
   She found her bridal roses at God's feet,
And now she walks in Heaven arrayed with them :
   She met me there with kisses close and sweet.
Oh ! one such meeting doth the grave disarm,
And break the wand of death and end his charm.

Then, trembling into distance, like a flower
   Dissolved in its own fragrance, or a kiss
That hives its sweetness for some coming hour,
   She vanished in the light of bosom bliss,

While Zapthalim drew near, and with him one
Called " Helios, the Angel of the Sun."

He wore white plumes pale as the soul of day ;
   Vesture as of the birds of Paradise
In gleamy radiance on his bosom lay ;
   An opalescent glory filled his eyes ;
And all the spirits of an airy choir
Sang to the motion of that strange attire.

A crimson mantle, tremulous with light,
   Floated around him ; in its beams intense
An ever-changing rainbow met my sight ;
   And sweet, beyond the melody of sense,
Were the soft accents that within it rung,
And made all Heaven like one glad lover's tongue.

     Slowly the mists unrolled.
  That stranger took my hand into his own,
     Then bound me to his breast
  With beamy ardors of angelic love.
     He whispered, " Let us rise."
  Then Aldebaran opened to my sight.
  Her gleamy streets, with jewelled palaces,
  Were all one hive of teeming industry.

The chalice of an infinite content
Supplied to every heart the honeyed wine :
"This," cried my guide, "is God Messiah's land."

THE POET OF THE FALLEN STAR.

"Hear of the star that fell !
There was a mighty minstrel, called of old
Luteia, on that orb whose pendant fruit
Ripened when yet thy planet was a germ.
He sang the story of its blissful years,
Before the bosom of the universe
Reflected ought save purity and peace.
The Heaven of Aldebaran is his home :
He sings to us, in music, native born,
Whose words are pictures in the glowing air,
And doves in all the woodlands of the heart,
And cataracts of light, that cleave the hills
And vault themselves in rainbows, to exhale
　　In honeyed incense-drops
　　And feed the laughing flowers.

"But love him for his heart.
Within the nectar of the wells of prayer

He lives, a hermit of the sacred years;
A messenger of God from star to star.
   Poet of Nature he,
And wanders through the universe of worlds,
And chronicles the ages by their bloom.
His soul is tuneful as a Doric flute,
With God Messiah's fingers on its keys,
   And breathing out His love.

"In Aldebaran we have many men
Who ripen as the mountains in their place;
Each one might be the genius of a world:
But this sweet singer moves among them all,
In lonely sacredness of element,
Beloved, revered and welcomed, but esteemed
The man of mystery.   He journeys on
Chanting a strain of power, that, when they hear
Trances the soul in wonder.   Lo! he comes.

   "Poet of Nature, he!
In his large heart the pictured years unroll:
His elements unite with all mankind,
   Upon thy wandering sphere,
   Who love the good and true.
Between him and his brother, Lucifer,

The dreadful gulfs of moral evil roll.
His brother fell, but he, a martyr, yea,
The first who met the murderous blade of sin,
And, dauntless, in his great allegiance, trod
To the first grave wherein man ever lay,—
He, bathed in atmospheres of sabbath bliss,
Through universal space, like morning fair
When it first blushes o'er a new-born world,
  Survives to tell the tale.

  " Poet of Nature, he,
And Nature's God, who, in him, syllables
The oracles of love. He is alone,
Set on the pillar of his martyred state,
Holding the sacred Word in his right hand,
Which, changeful yet unchanged, with tongues of fire,
Chants from within itself while God inspires.
Upon his brow a martyr-crown is set
Of dreadful agony, to such delight
Transformed, and all intensified, that one
Who gazes on it in his bosom burns,
Its mystery to fathom. There uplift,
In sacred wonder and astonishment,
His panoramic melodies expand :—
But he is gentle as a new-born child ;

The mildest of the **Angels** call him friend;
And many nations, with a long delight,
Uprear memorial pillars to his name.
Oh! many orbs unborn shall yet declare
That martyr's tuneful story; he shall be
Known by thy world, while tribes and peoples thrill
With spiritual fires of love divine,
   And blinded anarchs reel
   In sin's expiring hour,
Smit' in their breasts with quenchless agonies,
   When Heaven to earth descends.

  " Poet of Nature, he,
And Nature's first religion, which was peace.
He drank nepenthe on the hills of God,
With seers and sages, in his holy youth;
For he was, from his guileless infancy,
A welcome pilgrim of that inner shrine
Where Angels keep their watch above the worlds.
His kingly brother, tongued with martial flame,
Spoke to command; within his potent breast
Twelve constellations gathered up their beams;
   And, darkly, when he fell,
Gehenna lifted up her fiery front,
And cried, ' Who calls me? I am Misery!
   I was not, and I am!'

" Poet of Nature, he !

Upon his fair white brow is traced a name,

Which none may know save Him who wrote it there.

Come with me, thou shalt look upon his face.

Concentre all thy mounting **faculties,**

And, should he thunder from his pillared height,

Re-echo it in music to mankind.

    Thy grossness all must burn

Into its element and pass away ;

Thy essences consume with fervent heat ;

The palaces, wherein terrestrial thought

    Feeds on the baser dust,

In beaming splendors must dissolve ; the robes,

That mortals of thy orb delight to wear,

Melt in transparent whiteness ; and depart

All from thy spirit which cold worldlings **prize,**

Resolved to dreadful images of shame,

    As in the day of doom.

" Fear not, my brother, but rejoice to meet

The Poet whom thou seekest.   Let thy face

Blanch not before that fiery pediment,

Around whose **base ten** thousand cressets **flame,**

Each kindled when some young world first was made

    Love's holy nuptial bower.

Twelve symbol constellations round it roll,
Twelve vortices of light, in fiery seas.
Twelve mystic altars, three on either side,
        Bear the Deific name.
Peace and farewell! but where the brazen wall,
O'ertopped with flaming cherubim, appears,
A man shall meet thee by a gate of pearl:
Tell him thou comest at Messiah's call."

———

As when Elijah, in the chariot driven,
    Was parted from his friend, who stood below,
And lifted by the whirlwind into Heaven,
    That Angel left me, on my path to go:
On either side I heard the sound of waters,
White as the bosoms of Luteia's daughters.

In these far paths, that mildest Angels know,
    The symbols of the one religion shine
In sumptuous gardens, where the fruit-trees grow
    From inward elements of love divine;
And all its truths, arrayed on either hand,
Are living statuary, calm and grand.

Before my vision shone a ruby hill,
    Isled in a sea of luminescent pearl.

Fanning the air, with pinions never still,
   Were birds of molten flame : anon the whirl
Of a swift vortex lifted me : I stood
In ether borne above that wondrous flood.

The air itself was full of deathless thought
   Which had become substantial, and, to me,
A pantheon of art in visions wrought ;
   Or as the veil of God's eternity
Lest man should wither at his burning face ;
But in that air I felt a friend's embrace,

Who lifted me still higher, till the clearness
   Of angel-insight in my spirit nursed
A faculty to gaze with inward nearness ;
   Then myriad voices thrilled me with a burst
Of stately music, and the melody
Grew to a flamy car upbearing me,

Where a sublime quadrangle met my sight,
   Of burnished brass, and, by the middle door,
An Angel stood in flowing robes bedight.
   I bowed my head that mighty mind before,
And, when he asked me by what power I came,
Made answer, In the God Messiah's name.

At this the golden trumps began to blow
　　Held by the cherubim above the walls.
Then mounted on a white horse, all aglow
　　With morn's arising radiance, when she calls
The dreaming world from slumber, pure as arc
The heaven-beams that unite to shape a star,

Came Regina, the Angel of sweet dreams,
　　The Pilot Angel, watcher from afar
Of such, as, all intent on sacred themes,
　　Whom Earth's illusions have no power to bar,
Ascend in spirit o'er the orb's decay;
And she became conductress of my way.

A second steed, like spotless alabaster,
　　Shod with white opals, breathing through his mouth
Perfume like that once poured before the Master,
　　Approached: pale flowers, that love the balmy south,
Were woven in the tresses of his mane:
Silent he stood: then, speaking in a strain

Of inward sweetness, Regina rejoiced.
　　"Come, thou expected one," she cried: uplifted
I sat upon the white steed, many-voiced,
　　And, in its love, my heart with power was gifted

M

To pass in triumph through that stately door :
Within it shone a light unknown before,

As if the spirits of the atmospheres
 Had held **their** cups beneath Messiah's eyes,
When He is glad to wipe away the tears
 From dying martyrs, who to Heaven arise,
And poured the beams through beds of endless flowers,
Gemmed with the radiance of the morning **hours.**

Breathing the fragrance of that gleaming mist
 I fed my heart **on** odors rich as love.
Sublime, in stainless heavenly amethyst,
 Where twelve swift rainbows wreathed the vault above,
High **on his pillar stood that Martyr Man,**
And thus in stately speech his tale began.

   ———

" **With** Christ the God begins and ends my story ;
 Therefore this column stands, **a** monument
Of our Messiah's everlasting glory.
 I burn with Deity.   His voice hath lent
Such power as fills the floods, when they awake,
Unto my being : from your silence break,

" In **choral** thunders, ye reposeful nations,
 Who, in blue domes of crystal undefiled,

Worship amidst unfallen constellations;
  And bow thy head, thou pale poetic child,
In awful homage: I the theme rehearse
How Sin, the serpent, pierced the universe.

" I was a man born to a fair estate:
  Abaddon was my brother, and he grew
To his vast prime, an omniarch, elate
  With knowledges of power, and, ere the dew
Of youthful morn fled his pellucid eyes,
His soul had cleft the vaulted centuries.

" The planet was his mirror, where he saw,
  Reflected back in images of sense,
Form, origins and being; by the law
  Of the soul's growth, his cosmic mind, intense,
In ardors of perception sought the dim
Star spaces, where the ruling Cherubim

" Shadow their burning faces from God's throne.
  Twelve constellations, when his mother lay
In Hymen's nuptial house with unloosed zone,
  Wove for the unborn mind, in mystic play,
Twelve planes of faculties for each degree
Of the stupendous man that was to be.

" From the blissful dreams of his airy fold
  Canopus fed him with fruits of gold,
  Till his eyes were like lamps, with an inward fire,
  That turn to the steps of the solar choir ;
  And he slept like a moth in its moving rings,
  While its thoughts are unfolding to rapid wings ;
  And his nights were all trances, with light astir:
  They called him ' the Dawn-child' and ' Lucifer.'

" He grew with a veil o'er his hidden heart :
  He walked in his trance from our kind apart ;
  While the beams of the air in their flight stood still,
  And the primates of matter obeyed his will.
  And this was my brother: he swept by day
  Like a river whose waves with the sunbeams play ;
  While the gleam of his eyeball, to aid his cause,
  Held a magic more sure than the lion's jaws :
  He spoke with the might of the hidden mind,
  And his touch could loose, and his breath could bind.—
  Lonely I stand on a height untrod,
  Chanting for ever his fall from God.

" Where Orion walks with his burning brand
  Stands a Lion Star o'er an orbéd land.
  On this lion's head is a crown for kings,
  And he moves through space with an eagle's wings.

" 'Tis the Star of Fortune, the Star of Fame,
'Tis the Star of kings, who have built their name
In the music and motion of thought divine;
And Lucifer slept in its hidden shine.
O the Lion Star! when he felt its force,
His nerves throbbed full as a river course,
When the ocean rises to overbrim
Its valleys.   Alas for the fate of him!

———

" From Aldebaran's shadow vast
    The Poet's mantle o'er him fell,
And round his tranceful spirit cast
    First-born Elysia's lyric spell.
Oh Poet star! oh star of Love!
    First in the far celestial train,
Thou didst by night dissolve above
    Young Lucifer thy golden rain,
Thy honey-dew of blissful dreams,
    Thy crimson sparks from Hymen's pyre;
And, from thy pure concentred beams,
    He led the orb's resounding choir;
But walked apart, a lonely man,
    Till, in self-chosen madness whirled,
He dared the pure All-Father's ban,
    And, in his ruin, crushed a World.

" Thou hast vanished from thy height,
    Mistress of a sphere's delight ;
  On thy crescent fell a blight,
                        Oriana !   Oriana !

" Half thy race in ruins fell.
    I, for aye, thy story tell,
  Lonely where the Angels dwell :
                        Oriana !   Oriana !

" Thou wert built the hall of kings :
  O'er thy grave no planet swings :
  Madness to thine essence clings,
                        Oriana !   Oriana !

" Outcast of the starry fold,
    None thy palace-lights behold.
  Thou wert blotted out of old,
                        Oriana !   Oriana !

" Thou, who wert once a dovelet, then
    Became a wingéd serpent, when
  To demons turned thy planet-men,
                        Oriana !   Oriana !

" Lost Paradise, beside the streams
  Of morning, now a vulture screams

In thy soft breast of tender dreams,
>> Oriana! Oriana!

" Before, thou wert a matron mild :
Thou didst bring forth a kingly child,
Who, in his fall, thy couch defiled,
>> Oriana! Oriana!

" He smites his heart with stormy force;
He makes his hell a flying curse,
And wars against the universe.
>> Oriana! Oriana!

" A Mightier than he is found,
Who hath that orb of anarchs **bound.**
Resound, ye Heavens, with joy resound :
>> Oriana! Oriana!

" I journey where the Angels are,
And, from that fearful night, unbar
The story of the fallen star,
>> Oriana! Oriana!

" Lost planet of a sunken sea,
Within thy foundered argosy
A serpent seeks to smite at me,
>> Oriana! Oriana!

" He pierced me, when, with demon pride,
   The Spirit Father he defied :—
   I was the first who ever died :—
              Oriana !   Oriana !

" From star to star the burden ran,
   ' Man hath destroyed his brother man.'
   On me the war of hate began :—
              Oriana !   Oriana !

" I rose, by God uplifted, free,
   But, in my heart, the agony
   Moves on, transformed to melody :—
              Oriana !   Oriana !

" Never again, while ages roll their flight,
   Shalt thou regain thy throne of morning light,
   Lost anarch, wailing from thy ruin's night,
             ' Oriana !   Oriana !'

" Thy place shall be forgotten, Lucifer !
   Thy soul become its own dim sepulchre,
   When suns and systems end their moan for her.—
              Oriana !   Oriana !"

Part Third.

REGINA:

A SONG OF MANY DAYS.

REGINA:

A Song of Many Days.

HYMEN'S TRANSFIGURATION.

IN MEMORIAM.
JOHANNES KEATS.

PRELUDE.

UNDERNEATH these meadow daisies,
Hid away from human praises,
While his essence, pure and fine,
Glides through heavenly crystalline,
Lies a poet's earthly mould:
He for truth was wise and bold,
And the pansies of his eyes
Are as blue as any skies;
And the roses at his mouth

Crimson from the honeyed south.
Little thinks the bee, who sips,
He **is** feeding from the lips
That with Muses' nectar **ran,**
Love to God and love to man.

Love-lies-bleeding, at his heart,
Stings the air with honeyed smart,
Mixed with camomile, that grew
Where the venomed shaft ran through :
Fragrant, o'er the body's mound,
Thrives the plant, in gardens found,
That, beneath the spoilers' **feet,**
Groweth brave and smelleth sweet.

Virgin tuberose, plant of price,
Hymen's rod in Paradise,
From his bosom's middle space
Sanctifies the lowly place,
With a fragrance too intense
For a less than bridal sense.
Songs are hidden in its sweets
Latent in the soul of Keats,
Waiting for some nuptial morn,
From fresh kisses to be born.

I am glad that I am here,
This immortal tuberose near,
For I find, within it hid,
Thoughts, that through his bosom slid,
Rarer than ripe muscadine,
Vintage of Apollo's vine.—
King Apollo swept for him
Heaven's great lyre, and, in the dim
Twilight of an age to be,
Sowed his grave with melody.

From the dust, that was his breast,
Grows the plant I love the best,
Myrtle, chaplet for the dead,
Dying purely, all unwed,
And, with bride-lamp still unlit,
Gathered to the Infinite.

Holy dust of poet Keats,
Syllable, in lettered sweets,
Thoughts that Shelley half divined,
Thoughts to sow this passing wind.
I am sure there must be here
Loving words the world to cheer,
For the half embodied verse,

Hid within the pluméd hearse,
That with mother earth was blent,
Seeks its own bright element :
'Tis this myrtle flower to-day ;
Soon it will exhale away,
Lost upon forgetful air :
I must bind its essence rare.

He, I know, was all forlorn ;
For his verse he found a thorn.
Sweetest songs in time must fail,
Rose leaves wither on the gale ;
But his being, all too soon,
Vanished, like the setting moon,
Shorn of half its lily-white
Crescent by obscuring night.

I will pluck a plume, that came
From his wingéd Phœnix flame,
With Sabean spices fed,
And, upon this thymy bed,
Look into my heart, and write
Words that tremble with delight ;
While our poet's name shall be
So embalmed in melody,

That, as on an altar fair,
Carved in crystal shining air,
Linked with all things rich and rare,
Crowned for angel-bridals there,
Vast in joy as in despair,
He shall be the Muses' heir.

But I cannot write it, till
King Apollo's love-birds trill
In the woodlands of my breast;
And the sorrows that infest,
Like pale winter clouds o'erblown,
Leave my heart a summer zone:
In my being then shall be
Some diviner Castaly.

Come, thou blissful Lily Queen,
Trance me earth and heaven between;
Or, in pinnace all of smiles,
Float me to those Halcyon isles
Where the very air is sown
With the songs the Angels own;
Songs that warble as they glide
To thy happy heart, my bride,
Changing there to fairies all,
In some close embowered hall,

And, in hymeneal glee,
Weaving spells of minstrelsy.

King Apollo's golden bees,
Tangled in the summer breeze,
Like the Pleiades in their net,
Known by starry sparkles yet,
Fairest fingers I will find
Your enchantment to unbind:
Fairies, from the coral lips
And the rosy finger tips,
Shall unloose your flying veil :
Then, when Eve is twilight-pale,
And the starry lawns are spread
O'er us like a daisy bed,
When the souls of joys unborn
Float between the night and morn,
Underneath the argent white
Of the young moon's bridal night,
From the mother and the child,
From the virgin pure and mild,
From the hero-hearts that keep
War with Wrong in very sleep,
From the soft and lucid eyes,
Lit with gleams of Paradise,
From white bosoms pillowed still

In forgetfulness of ill,
Nursing all a fairy choir
In the gladness they inspire,
Ye shall bring ambrosial balm,
Sweet as drops from Syrian palm:
Then the liquid strain shall melt,
With a rapture inly felt,
Till the listening mind is led
Where **the lyric boy is** wed.

HYMEN'S TRANSFIGURATION.

From sweetest lips we gather, while we may,
Sweets for remembrance in an after-day.
The joys we taste, like cloistered nuns enshrined,
Live on, pale hermits of the pensive mind.
The nuptial eve is there transformed, and made
The soft Enchantress of the moonlit glade.
Blisses **too** brief, that long ago befell,
Blush like Rebecca at the dripping well.
As through dim night the rosy dawn we see,
From joys that were we paint futurity.

So, when great Poets, nobler than their verse,
Embalmed in music vanish, and the hearse

N

Hides the sweet singer, while in heart we sigh
That one of deathless thought himself should die,
They take their place, in some pure shrine we rear,
With crowned Immortals to all memory dear :
The robe of song, that, royally, they cast,
In their translation, floats in ether vast,
And new Elijahs cross the lyric sea,
Clad in its brightness, to eternity.

O joy that was ! our Keats, whose buds of song
Are bridal memories for ages long,—
Whose verses blush, with mild lips unreproved,
As thou in Heaven to find thyself beloved,
And, like fresh eglantine when hawthorns fail,
Renew **the** amorous beauty of **the** vale,
And **oft** prolong, into December night,
The year's young fragrance and its first delight,—
From thy sweet lays what wondrous plants arise,
To climb the kindling spirals of the skies !

The tender songs, in earth that have their root,
Ripen above to all delicious fruit.
The rosy apples of delight are **born**
From melodies, that yielded here the thorn ;
While lays, that knew their birth in Love Divine,
Flower for aye in Heaven's red morning-shine.

Sad Poesy, that here, an infant, slept
In the lone heart; or died, a child unwept;
Or vanished, like the incense that exhales
From half-blown roses when the Summer fails;
An airy form, to spiritual sense,
Claims its new birthright, born from the intense
And wedded ardors of the Minstrel's breast;
Through heavenly innocence becomes a blest
And wingéd creature sportive as the fay;
Finds in the skies its atmospheres of play,
And feeds itself with all melodious things,
From every joy divine Elysium brings.

So Milton owned his Paradise Regained;
A prisoned Epic here, in bonds enchained;
An eyeless hero toiling at the bars :—
He robed himself in gladness from the stars,
And rose, in rapture, o'er the realms of space;
Then, from his heart-queen's beautiful embrace,
Through every vein the fluent music ran :—
Full song requires the fulness of the man.

So Dante, when he rose, with new found breath,
To clasp the Angel where he thought the Death,
Turned in his bliss from human themes apart,

N 2

Tasting the blisses of the wedded heart,
Till Beatrice touched the vocal keys
And woke within the vaster harmonies.
How sweet it was, in morning bliss, to find
The Muse, the Angel and the Wife combined!
"Forget the past," he cried, "thou heart be still;
Drink of pure silence thine enamored fill;
Steep the lost laurel in forgotten tears;
Voiceless the myrtle blooms to crown the years."

But no! the rest, the rapture and the ray
Revived the Genius of the solemn lay.
A new Comedia rose, with wings of fire,
Plumed from the ardors that the **blest respire**;
And the great theme, on dreary earth begun,
Transfigured shone beneath the Spirit Sun.

SONG.

I.

THE Meadow Daisy came to me
And said, 'I perish silently,
And fade away from space:

But rise, transformed, an airy flower,
Beneath the vine leaves of a bower,
 Shrine for an Angel-grace.'

II.

The modest Celandine drew nigh,
And whispered, with a gentle sigh,
 ' Dear friend, forget me not.
I bloom again, exhaling rare
Deliciousness for Angel fair:
 Mine is a blessed lot.'

III.

The happy Pansy spoke, and smiled,
' Beloved I am by every child,
 And prized by maiden dear.
Thou too shalt find me, poet friend,
In gardens that the Muses tend,
 What time I disappear.'

IV.

Then the red Rose approached, and wept
Her fragrance to a cloud, that slept
 At nightfall in my breast;

But, from the odor, sprang a tree,
Wherein the happy rose, for me,
   In crimson bloom was dressed.

V.

The Tuberose o'er a little mound,
Close to a poet's head-stone found,
   Wafted intense delight :
A maiden drank it in a breath ;
It rose again, from seeming death,
   With robes of virgin light.

VI.

Oh heart! I cried, the sight behold :
The Lovely never groweth old,
   It never sees decay ;
But floats to some supernal star,
And lives where the Immortal are ;
   Meet for their nobler day.

VII.

The poet's thought drops down, a seed,
Wafted to hearts that little heed :
   Perchance a day of care

Weeps o'er its dust in tearful rain ;—
A sweet distress, a tender pain,
  It blooms transfigured there.

VIII.

Oh flower beloved! Oh blissful song!
Forgotten once, remembered long,
  Thou shalt from time **depart,**
Borne upward in the soft caress,
And blooming in the tenderness
  Of the Ascending Heart!

———

Ah, happy Eve! in some close **bowered nook,**
When crimson rose-leaves shower upon the book,
Graced by a pure and all too-loving lay
For aught save young brides on their nuptial day ;—
For joy-songs too intense, in heart reborn,
Flutter to find impalement on a thorn!
The young moon, in a scarf of silver air,
Veils her white breast and hides the lilies there :
We start :—the soul wakes with a sudden thrill;
The sun and moon of inner life stand still :
Young Love first meets the fair Ideal then,
And we are blest beyond the sons of men.

But, **when** the first, fond, answered glance is o'er,
And the heart's rose-tree reddens to the core,
We tremble, inwardly, to know Delight,
Like young Narcissus, blushing from the sight.
In Vision's well, by secret charm divined,
He meets, unveiled, his fairer heart and mind.
Then all of Paradise we first believe,
When the Soul's Adam thrills at conscious **Eve,**
Our better self, in finer grace arrayed :—
The viewless beams of her sweet life pervade
The breast, that burns **to** claim the breathing joy ;
While the maid's love is wisdom in the boy.

Ah happy time ! the pulse of young desire
Throbs inly, fed by no material fire.
Fain would we blend, as ray combines with ray,
And glide, entranced, beyond the ebbing day.
Heaven floats before us then with no disguise,
Seen through the veiled enchantment of her eyes,
While the queen maiden, with some threefold rod,
Wakes the Heart's angel to commune with God :—
Eve lost her spouse his paradise of old,
But we our Eden through the mate behold.

She turns : she lingers : it is growing late :

Impatient friends call at the garden gate :
One bashful glance she gives, and glides away :—
But Memory lives when we are old and gray.
Yes, Memory lives, and opes, with golden key,
The bridal chamber of eternity.—
Who was the maiden? " But a stranger guest."
Where is she now?—we pause in vague unrest,—
Gone, beauteous passage bird, without a trace :—
Ah! but our hearts, thank God, they still embrace.

She dies.   We know it.   How? in solemn trance
The earth recedes, the viewless ones advance :
She floats, transfigured, o'er the dust, that shone
With an effulgent beauty not its own.
Henceforth, whate'er the labors of our lot,
Heaven holds our Angel, earth enthralls us not.
A silent music haunts the pillowed night,
A gliding joy-form, robed in lucid light,
Whispers of some diviner land apart,
Veiled for the nuptials of the pure in heart.

Or she is found.   Then every blossom courts,
And hall and bower seem made for happy sports.
Again the new moon shews her silver horn ;
But Being's hill-tops burn with glowing morn.

What dovelets coo in that reposeful breast?
To the Soul's thought she seems an essence, dressed
In beauty, woven from the heart's delight,
Kindred to air and flame and morning light,
Rich fruits, bright flowers and songs by poets made :
Half in the soul's light, half in body shade,
She flits, too joyous for the asking sense,—
A Woman-child, a regal Innocence.

So, to young Burns, that Highland Mary came,
Enrobed, for him, in morn's translucent flame ;
Enchanted maiden, hallowing the cot
With hidden charms, by earth imagined not ;
Veiled in soft dreams, of airy tissue spun ;
Gliding, perchance, to Venus or the Sun ;
Weaving, within that beautiful disguise,
The peerless form that ripens in the skies.
Ah! 'twas no fancy : with a pure content,
The Woman-angel of his Jacob tent,
Through the rude self the Lyric Soul to find,
She roused the sleeper, to his genius blind ;
Then fled, to bloom, complete, in heavenly bliss,
Ere the Immortal won the bridal kiss.

SONG.

I.

THAT Poet's Muse is little worth
Who rhymes for ever of the earth:
With filmy wings the bat may sail,
But ne'er will be the nightingale:
Divinely sing of things divine;
So shall true poet's gift be thine.

II.

Sell not thy gold for foolish dross:
Nail not thy God-gift on the cross:
Let not the senses cheat thine eye,
Thou child and pilgrim of the sky!
But sing, though worldlings close their ears:
Thine are the hymns of all the spheres.

III.

To fearless virtue Heaven is kind.
Poets, who leave their age behind,
And climb the mountain peaks of thought,
Where choral thunders first are wrought,
May tune their souls to every key
Of regal ages yet to be.

IV.

Find in the soul those shining stairs
That saints have trod, through noblest cares,
And thou shalt reach the mystic door
Incarnate Love has oped before.
There bloom the true Elysian fields,
Where every leaf a lyric yields.

But we are wed.   Shine forth, in blissful noon,
Sun of the Angels ! **gild** the honey-moon.
The hallowed stillness of the bridal night
Reveals a maiden, robed in airy **white.—**
Was it a dream,—with new found gladness rife,
The husband saw the Spirit of the wife,,
With Hymen's nectar cup,—a vision dim,—
Brimmed from All-Father, bending over him.

What new Correggio shall live to paint
The sacred beauty of the wedded saint,
The Bride-girl, who, from Hymen's Heaven, brings down
The lily sceptre and the red rose crown?
Ah ! well may Heaven, with more than mother care,
Guard the soft slumbers of the tender pair.
Clasped hand in hand, the two-in-one ascend :—

Sweet song, rise with them to their journey's end.
What purer breath pervades the bosom now?
What nobler morning lights the regal brow?
What radiant bridegroom leads the blooming spouse,
To taste the cheer of Hymen's golden house?
What veiled affection lives in every grace,
Where truth and goodness claim the long embrace?
From that full joy what thoughts divine have birth,
When bride and bridegroom wake once more on earth.

SONG.

FOR E. M. W.

I.

THE Bride-star, in a long eclipse,
Pales here, from mute impassioned lips,
   And eager, asking eyes:
O maiden with the golden hair!
I entered the Third Heaven, and there
   Beheld the planet rise.

II.

Enveiled in soft suffusive beams,
From the glad light of blissful dreams,

It floated on from space;
And in it shone a kingly pair,
As Morning bright, as Evening fair,
    Tranced in a long embrace.

III.

The cohorts of the burning host
Thrilled, as the star, belovéd **most,**
    Star of the two-in-one,
Sped eastward, to exhale from sight,—
A cataract of living light,—
    A rainbow round the Sun.

IV.

O maiden of the dove-like heart!
Beloved, revered, where'er thou art,
    Whose nuptials now portend;
For thee the visioned arch was lit,
Thine was the orb, and, shrined in it,
    The Spirit of my friend.

V.

A better Hymen **than the slow,**
Reluctant genius mortals know,
    Shall grace thy bridal board :

Fill the heart's cup with festal wine;
'Twill brim for thee to love divine;—
Thy Hymen is the Lord!

———

O beauteous bride, what blissful years have shed
Their 'soft consenting fulness' on thy head?
Thy vows were made, thy marriage joy-bells rung,
Perchance, when the grand century was young.
Pause at these mortal boundaries of space,
This lingering twilight of the earth-born race;
Inheritress of empires all to be,
Seen through the sunset, what appears to thee?
Say, is the heart, with teeming life astir,
A veiled Elysium or a sepulchre?
Are these the morning or the evening rays,
That on the Pisgah mount of Vision blaze?
Is that far land, whose avenues, to me,
Ray from the presence of Divinity,
And all converge, where all delights are known,
In life's intensity around the throne,—
Is it, or is it not, the promised goal?
Young Love divined thy bridal home, thou soul!

The pure Departed, of the ages gone,
They gleam, they smile, they pause, they beckon on.
Perchance the veteran, seamed with noble scars,—

His triumphs told by crosses and by stars,—
The gray-haired man beside thee, will confess
If thy pure lip hath still the power to bless.—
Ah! is it so? 'I tremble to her still,
O poet, as the ice-bound woodlands thrill
When Spring glides by, with warm enamored breath,
To stir the pulses from their seeming death;
And, when the body's gates, by night ajar,
Reveal the wonders of the land afar,
Where the Great Captain numbers o'er His host,
And those are worthiest found who loved the most,
The Bridal Angel smiles, her youth to see,
In the still waters of eternity.'

SONG.

I.

Look up, my Love! the twilight star
  Shines o'er the hill-top yonder:
There, two-in-one, in Hymen's car,
  At last our souls may wander.

II.

The bridal crescent, here that wanes,
  An endless light, is given,

Where Hymen pipes his dulcet strains,
   Upon the hills of Heaven.

III.

'Tis true, sweet wife, we're growing old.
   The daisies of the meadow
Will blossom soon, above our mould,
   Deep in the church-yard shadow :

IV.

But, hand in hand, we'll journey on,
   Through Autumn's cloudy weather,
Till Hymen's Better Land is won :—
   We're growing young together.

V.

Look up, my Love ! the evening star
   Shines o'er the hill-top yonder.
In its Arcadian vales afar
   Our spirits yet may wander.

———

Lost Youth stands waiting on the Summer shore :
Lost loveliness re-blooms, to fade no more :
The Soul, in that immortal second birth,
Wakes in the Heaven it built itself on earth ;

O

Its church, the faith-act through the century grown,
With all the graces in resplendent stone :
Prayer, the veiled artist, on the soul's deep keys,
Beethoven-like awakes the symphonies,
And the still music, crystallized above,
Reveals the wisdom of its inmost love.
Pause here, thou Muse! 'tis night; respire with me
This fragrance of the rose and citron tree.
A sleeping saint enjoys the deep repose,
That, through the bosom, from All-Father flows.
What flowers are these, unseen, that still have fed,
With bridal thoughts, the chaste reposeful bed?
And ah! they open now : what ravished ears
Since Plato fled, have heard your hymn, ye Spheres?
'Tis the Soul's song, in low, sweet undertone,
That listening Angels might delight to own.
This shall declare how, in its glory, stands
Yon mansion, built by virtues, not by hands.

SONG.

I.

I BUILD my house of loving deeds,
On Christ, the mighty corner stone,

And, when for love my spirit bleeds,
   I find a ruby chamber grown.

II.

I build my house of tender cares :
   My daily labors, great or small,
Are pearly gates and golden stairs,
   Into Messiah's banquet hall.

III.

I build my house of soul-desires,
   And, where the secret prayers arise,
They wind aloft in stately gyres,
   To Angel-gardens in the skies.

IV.

I build my house with Satan's blows :
   He smites my Master through my breast.
In every wound a streamlet flows,
   With wine and honey of the blest.

V.

I build my house of silent tears,
   For human hearts with sorrow riven ;
In each a crystal pane appears,
   And makes a window into Heaven.

VI.

I build my house of Christ confest;
  The work is His, the joy is mine;
He smoothes the pillow of my rest,
  And bids me in His arms recline.

―――

A shining company have lit, afar,
The bridal lamps in yon celestial star.
Old man, methinks, with feeble steps and slow,
Thou ploddest o'er the bleak December snow.
Where the lost honeymoon? the bashful bride?
Where! in thee, o'er thee, moving on beside.
Come, little fairy, once a darling, born
Of still heart-nuptials, firstling of the morn,
Fled where the spirits of the rose and bee
Dwell on the lyric hills of Arcady,—
Thou blissful grace, whose airy being, spun
Of mirth and music, sought the Fairy Sun,
And, kindling there to pure immortal flame,
An angel-fay of the Heart's Heaven became,—
Sing, in the bosom where thy essence nursed,
In wifely joy, its wee fay-babies first,
Why the lone pilgrim his cold way beguiles
With whispered words, and tender, child-like smiles?

Why innocence delights to find his breast,
Caressing still though haply uncaressed?
His weary senses seem by age to fail;
From life he turns as from a thrice-told tale.
"Ah!" cries the fairy, "fairies are his friends;
To fairyland the second childhood tends."

beauti

SONG.

I.

TheY hallow the air
  With a music rare,
And around his mind they spin,
  Than the sun and the moon
  More bright, the cocoon
Of the trance they fold him in.

II.

Of the second life,
  And the blooming wife,
They chant, with a golden chime,
  From the joy-bells, rung
  When his heart was young,
And the twain were in their prime.

III.

So he dreams apart,
    With a blissful heart,
And the patient fairies go,
    With a soft **refrain,**
    Through the quiet **brain,**
Till he floats from his lonely **woe:**

IV.

And he has no fears
    Of the leafless years,
Nor dread of their long decay ;
    But thrills **to the kiss**
    Of the coming **bliss,**
And the endless nuptial day.

———

Glad is the fay, who, for the maiden's bower,
Tints the red rose, perfumes the **orange flower;**
Glad is the bride, who sees, through happy tears,
In the heart's mirror, Hymen's golden years :
Thrice glad the youth who moves elate beside.—
Those golden years into their ocean glide.—
A pensive maiden waits, in Heaven apart,
Her bower the type and emblem of the heart ;

The stalactital walls, with morning lit,
Her prayers below that sought the Infinite;
Her deeds of mercy pictured everywhere,
Through curtained vistas of joy-breathing air;
Each meek self-sacrifice a statued Love,
From inward bliss melodious like the dove;
The days and nights, she spent in trials oft,
Made mossy carpets verdurous and soft;
While the still benedictions, that were sped
By her pure spirit thrill beneath the tread.
Mark ye that alcove, through dim twilight shewn?
Breathe low, sweet song! nor tremble at thy tone:
There, by the jewelled cressets, dimly fed
With odorous oils, shall bridal prayers be said:
There, floating upward through purpureal skies,
Shall praises to the heavenly Hymen rise:
There, in celestial purity enshrined,
The breathing Soul shall clasp the kindred Mind.
The bride-girl waits,—kind Heaven the scene allows,—
Thrilled by the joy-song of the coming spouse:
" Fly swift, thou rapid gondola of Time,
Moved by the heart-strokes of the will sublime;
Lessen the distance, cleave the flying sea :—
I thrill, I pant, sweet Innocence, for thee.
Unread the page the wingéd years unroll;

Futurity alone illumes the soul.
Thou art! and, as to Him my prayers ascend
Who guides the pinnace to its journey's end,
They find thee, Angel, greet thee on their way,
In thy glad bower with airy winglets play,
Then move, with thine, **where the world's praises meet,**
And fuse our spirits at Messiah's **feet.**

" Perish the doubt, the craven fear, that still
Would yield the issues of the race to Ill.
While Night, imperial giant, crowned with stars,
Forges the darts of Morning on his bars;
While Morn, effulgent, parts his regal robe
To gather to his breast the wedded globe;
I'll triumph o'er the terrors that await,—
The sable vista and the shrouded gate;
Those terrors but the shade, that noontide flings
Upon me from the great Archangel's wings;
That shroud the veiling Love, that would allay,
Awhile, the beams of all-effulgent day!
While Christendom uplifts, **with eager hands,**
The jewelled cup, her nobler Genius stands,
And fills the goblet, centuries a-dry,
With fiery draughts of immortality !"

SONG.

I.

Thou art nearer than a brother, O Thou Friend of all
    mankind!
All who ask Thy grace receive it; all who crave Thy pre-
    sence find.
To the loving Thou descendest, and art evermore with them,
While they walk, by faith beholding, in the New Jerusalem.

II.

Where the feet of watching Angels make the ways of
    darkness bright,
Where the comforts of Thy promise temper anguish with
    delight,
Where the fruit trees bloom around us and the little chil-
    dren laugh,
There are traces of Thy presence, there are tokens of Thy
    path.

III.

Thou art bending o'er the lilies when they burgeon from
    the sod,
And each pure corolla sparkles in the radiance of God;

Where the tiny violets perfume, with **their sweets, the
forest lea,**
In the spirit of their fragrance is a breathing out of Thee.

IV.

All the **world** is very **holy : Thou art** here, as once of old,
When **the** Angels hailed Thine **advent while** they smote
their harps of gold.
With our spirit-eyes we see Thee, when **Thou comest to us**
now,
With the crowns **of earth and** heaven in the glories of **Thy
brow.**

V.

Thou art Poet to the poets ; when **Thy love attunes their**
lyres,
They may chant for all the nations, **while** Messiah-God
inspires.
Thou art Hero to the heroes ; when for **love** alone they
smite,
Thou, above them, dost emblazon **the broad** oriflamme of
light.

VI.

Thou art Martyr to the martyrs, when in secret woes they
bleed,

Passing o'er the burning ploughshares while they sow the
    holy seed.

Thou art Lover to the lovers, when the two Thou makest one

Blend their hearts in chaste espousals, like Immortals in
    the sun.

VII.

Not a breast that breathes for mercy, but Thy blessings
    overflow :

Thou art moving o'er the spirit, as the pleasant south winds
    blow :

As the sun its rays attempers, when it beams for human
    eyes,

Thou dost shine on human nature from the blessed inner
    skies.

VIII.

From the fulness of Thy being, o'er the humble, thou hast
    poured

Fiery tongues of men and Angels, inspirations of Thy
    Word ;

And our hearts, within us burning, while we trace the
    solemn page,

Read the glories of Thy kingdom in the Second Christian
    Age.

FINALE.

As blooms the lily of the field,
  This lyric blossom grew;
Fed by the grace the Spirit yields,
  For light and morning dew.

It is the harbinger of one,
  Whose coming is, to me,
As the ascension of the sun,
  Prefigured inwardly.

So, while the gentle Summer fades
  Upon these ruins old,
And deeper gloom the night invades,
  And heaven is clear and cold,

I take my pilgrim staff in hand,
  And close, with prayer and praise,
The book that king Apollo planned,
  The Song of Many Days.

Laund House: Bolton Abbey: England.
    August 31st, 1859.

SONGS

BY THE SEA SIDE.

———

TO G. W. S.

.

Songs

PROEM.

PAUSING, by this delicious shore,
I chant the songs that bubble o'er
   From some diviner sea,
   That ebbless flows in me.

Whence do the poet's thoughts descend,
To words of wingéd flame that tend,
   Or drop, in vocal rain,
   Upon the thirsty plain?

We are but instruments, that thrill,
Responsive to His lyric will,
   Who pours the seas, like sand,
   In sunshine from His hand.

FAREWELL TO SUMMER,
1859.

THE chimes of the lyrical Summer,
   The tones of the bird **and the** bee,
That tunefully met the **new-comer,**
   With airs of an infantile glee,
   Dissolve on the lips of the sea.

The mother-like ocean is **yearning,**
   The world with her pleasance to brim;
Like paths of **the Angels are burning**
   The rainbows that rest **on the rim,**
   With **mystical splendor and dim.**

What ships of the blessed are sailing,
   In light o'er the hyaline floor,
Afar in the sunset unveiling,
   Remote from the vapory shore;
   Soft visions, returning no more!

Young children, with Zephyr-like dances,
   They dimple the musical sands:
The ocean, with queenly advances,

Enfolds them in crystalline bands,
White roses and pearls from her hands.

The chimes of the lyrical Summer,
    The tones of the bird and the bee,
With rapture that met the new-comer,
    Revive on the lips of the sea;—
    Return, in glad echoes, to me.

My heart, on the breast of the ocean,
    Reclines in a tremulous rest;
It vibrates with musical motion;
    It chimes to the songs of the blest;
    It sings, of the Summer possest.

Here all things, that greet me, are emblems
    Of life, in the newness begun;
Yon ocean a radiant semblance,
    That rolls to the smile of the sun,
    Of peace that by loving is won.

Roll on, in thy beautiful being,
    Glad ocean, with music afar.
Life bears me to meet the All-seeing,
    Where all the beatified are,
    With space at my feet like a star.

WHITBY ABBEY.*

VEILED in a **dim and moonlit** mist,
   St. Hilda's Abbey stands,
Holding a broken crucifix
   Aloft in stony hands ;—
A phantom from the **night of years**,
   Dim o'er the Whitby sands.

Ah me ! **what** old traditions throng
   Around the holy place !
Hilda, the Saxon maiden, smiles
   In soft, seraphic grace ;
The bloom of love upon her cheek,
   Heaven's light above her face.

Here, **gay** with roof **of** summer green,
   Or white with winter snow,
The saintly virgin reared the walls
   Twelve centuries ago :

---

* The ruins of this ancient monastery **occupy** a conspicuous position upon the east cliff of Whitby, and for miles are visible, as a land-mark, on the German **Ocean.** The Abbey, according to the historians, was first erected by St. Hilda, **A.D. 658.** The venerable Bede recounts her death, as having been accompanied by **visions of the departure of the spirit to the** Heavens, in the society of Angels.

A mile afar the ocean, then,
 That murmurs now below.

Celestial woman, lo! she smiles
 Above the cloistered bar;
Or moves through azure space, elate,
 In dove-drawn angel car;
Or chants her endless bridal song,
 From Hymen's happy star.

'Tis said that, on the night she fled
 The body's hallowed shrine,
A Vision came, with steps of light
 And tender looks benign,
To sing her blessed soul's release
 To raptures all divine.

St. Hilda's Abbey moulders now
 Upon the sea-worn hill;
The bells, that rung the angelus,
 No more the vapors thrill;
But, through my heart, her happy soul
 Wafts down a blessing still.

———

WHITBY SANDS:

THE MARCH OF SUBVERSION.

GLAD uplands, where, in standing corn,
　　Gay reapers woke their Saxon glee,
Are crumbled now, to sands forlorn,
　　　　Beneath the swelling sea;

Type of undaunted will, that beats,
　　With fierce persistence, ever more,
And throbs, with pauseless tidal beats,
　　　　To smite the rugged shore;

Type of the stormy force, that wears
　　The Old, by time, nor e'er abates;
But lifts the stony walls, and bears
　　　　Afar the fortress gates!

The Peaceful vanishes away;
　　The moving Strife usurps its place;
The cliffs of hallowed Faith decay,
　　　　That girdled once the race:

But whither, whither, march they on,
    Whose steps are as the waters free?
The corn-fields of the Past are gone:
       What harvest bears the sea?

HEART-NEWNESS.

The Morning awakes in her chamber,
    The morn of a fairer state:
The seas of the sorrowful deluge
    Around my ark abate.

The storms of the terrible conflict
    Are melodies for my way,
As the snows of the chill December
    Return in the flowers of May.

Over the crimson hill-tops
    The homes of the Blest appear;
Their wonderful songs flow round me;
    Their beautiful words appear;

Words that are tinted landscapes,—
   Odor and light and love;
Songs that are swift affections,
   Plumed from the joys above.

ROBIN HOOD.

HERE, at Whitby Abbey, stood
Once the band of Robin Hood:
Merry archers, ye are gone,
Friar Tuck and Little John:
Soon the hollow shrine must fall,—
Headstone for you, one and all.

Sharpened quarrels that ye shot,—
Still the field is unforgot,—
Heap an airy monument
Underneath the azure tent.
This your pyramid shall be;
Crumbled now the greenwood tree.

Better, clad in Lincoln green,
Than with monkish gabardine,

Silent shades! ye softly go,
Where the Sun of long-ago
Shines, with visioned splendors, o'er
Memory's receding shore.

In an age when laws, that bless,
Served for pretexts to oppress,
Ye were England's freest part,
Nurselings of the Saxon heart;
Therefore here, on Whitby Hill,
Chants your fame the poet still.

ELEANORE.

THE LOVER'S WORDS AT THE DEATH BED.

She looks so fair, now she is dead,
The saintly maid I hoped to wed,
   That, from a storm of woes,
   I taste her still repose.

Her mother weeps and wrings her hands:
Her father like a statue stands;
   While, with enamored breath,
   Death sighs, and is not death.

A finger, to its fellows prest,
Shews, from the white snows of her breast,
    A ruby glistening;
     'Tis our betrothal ring.

Glad eve! with what a dreamy spell,
Veiled in fresh flowers, the fountain fell:
    Our hearts interpreted
     Their silent words, unsaid.

Dear one! as in a trance divine,
She watched the evening planet shine,
    Then, musical and low,
     Breathed, " Surely, it is so."

Tell me the thought, I spake, and she
Answered with sudden melody,
    And downcast maiden eyes,
     " Heart-union in the skies."

As when the full drop brims the rose,
My soul, with tender overflows
    Of pleading love, replied,
     Ah! wert thou but my bride,

Hereafter, when the gates unbar,
That close the death, and ope the star,
    My unborn angel-flame
    Would kindle, at thy name.

Ah! memory, be still, be still!
We heard the mother whip-poor-will,
    Teaching her callow young
    Their sweet, vibrating tongue.

As if my love-suit were unheard,
"List!" she rejoined, "the matron-bird,
    Ere the young brood have flown,
    Warbles their after-tone.

"These thrills and flutterings in the breast,
These auguries of wedded rest,
    When soul, commixt with soul,
    Speeds to the angel-goal,

"Are all the language that we learn,
Taught by the Mother Heavens, that yearn,
    With voices of heart-good,
    To wake their human brood.

'(Love is, on earth, a prophecy,) *bless God,*
That seeks fruition in the sky.   *it is.*
    Claim me, beloved! thy own
    At the great Lover's throne."

Take then, O Death! to-day thy part:
Thine the soft semblance, mine the heart.
    I wait,—'twill not be long,—
    I wait her bridal song.

DEATH OF THE FLOWERS.

THE clouds are cloistered arches:
    The winds pace to and fro,
Chanting their mournful aves:
    From hands of ice and snow
They drop their beads, and hailstones
    Fall to the earth below.

Death to the flowers of Autumn!
    The midnight mass is said:
Now Frost, the mitred abbot,
    With jewels on his head,

Puts forth his sparkling crozier,
  And lo! the flowers are dead.

Their tender hearts are broken:
  They drop their lives in seed,
Till Spring, the promised angel,
  Shall, with his golden reed,
Wake the imprisoned martyrs,
  The City of God to heed.

Four square, its vast foundations
  Shall glad their waking eyes;
Then all their buried nations
  Shall, thousand-fold, arise,
And wreathe, in Earth's fair temple,
  An altar for the skies.

THE RIVER ESK.

HERE, where the gentle river flows,
Through vallies in a soft repose;
Or coyly smiles, a Naiad queen,
To bind her brows with garlands green;

In land-locked waters of the bay,
　The Dane, with raven standard, lay.
The Dane is gone; in a mild repose
The river smiles as it seaward flows.

　Here, where the river ebbs and flows,
　Or dies into the blue repose,
　Or, with a tranquil murmur, laves
　St. Mary's hallowed mount of graves,
　The ruddy Saxon came, to spoil
　The pagan ancients of the soil.
The Saxon gone, in a mild repose
The river smiles as it seaward flows.

　Here, where the gentle river flows,
　Kissed by the summer wind that blows,
　While the tired fisher stirs to feel
　Her white hands heaving at the keel,
　The Roman strode along the strand,
　Or threw the discus on the sand.
Rome is no more! in a mild repose
The river smiles as it seaward flows.

　Time is a stream, that flows and flows,
　To meet eternity's repose.

The darkness fades; corrodes the chain;
The endless golden years remain.
The raven flies; returns the dove;
Flash o'er the waves the lights of love.
The river smiles, as it flows and flows,
To beautiful years of the world's repose.

INNOCENCE.

COME to me, O ye children!
　For I am a child once more;
And Nature, the wonderful poem,
　I read with an Angel's lore.

Ye pause with your glowing faces;
　Ye cease in your airy play;
At home with the birds and the blossoms,
　And blithesome and fresh as they.

Ye hear, in the heart's vibrations,
　·The song of the life before;
Deep as the sound in the sea-shells,
　That lie on the pebbled shore.

Come to me, O ye children!
   The shadow of self, that flies,
As clouds that obscure the landscape,
   Shall melt in the soft replies.

I float on the stream **where ye** dally,
   At play by the lilied marge;
I come and go o'er the waters,
   That swell to an ocean large.

I know where the sunset flieth,
   And where the red morn has birth;
Where the Beautiful builds her palace,
   Who vainly is sought on earth:

Where the fathers and mothers are **waiting,**
   Who dwelt **in** the long-ago;
Where the brothers and sisters **are** playing,
   Who passed through the church-yard snow.

I know **where the roses flourish**
   Ye gathered **and** cast away;
Where **the** innocent songs ye warbled
   Are birds, with a tender lay.

Come to me, O ye children!
  And see where the sleeper lies,
At the foot of the starry ladder,
  Between the earth and the skies.

THE CALL OF CÆDMON.*

CÆDMON, the Saxon peasant,
  At crucifix of stone,
Deep in the burning midnight,
  When darkness filled the throne,
  Knelt praying all alone.

With infinite sweet chorus,
  The drops of that mild rain,
That falls, in benedictions,

* Among the brethren of the religious house founded at Whitby was Cædmon, the most fervent and original of the Saxon bards. As tradition avers, he
was a peasant, residing near the Abbey. It was his custom to retire from feasts
invariably, before his turn for singing, having no faculty of lyrical utterance,
however rude. On one occasion of this sort he fled to the cattle-stalls and fell
asleep among the oxen. During the night a refulgent Person appeared to him
in a vision, and greeted him with, "Cædmon, sing Me something." The poem
follows the narrative. Cædmon awoke, a Poet, and became the Minstrel of the
Word to his nation.

On restful heart and brain,
Awoke a long refrain.

He thought of the All-Father,
And slept, **assoiled from** blame;
When, o'er enkindled **ocean**,
Wrapt in a moving **flame**,
The MAN he worshipped came.

Now Cædmon was no poet;
From feast and floor he fled,
Before his turn for singing;
And aye, with aching head,
Fell praying on his bed.

But this night something **deeper**,
Within his spirit, stirred,
Importunate, unceasing;
Like some vast ocean-bird:
Its wings were as the Word.

And moving, **ever** moving,
With sounds of a deep lyre,
The incense-dropping pinions
Fanned into flames the fire,
Within his bosom-pyre.

Then, spake the MAN resplendent,
  "Attune thy lips to glee."
With passionate tears he answered,
  "Songless from feast I flee."
  "Nay, Cædmon, sing for Me!"

O power of faith celestial!
  O miracle divine!
Sweet as the new metheglin,
  The Saxon's honeyed wine,
  Flowed the enraptured line.

SURPRISES.

THE midnight of a good man's life
With sudden light, from Heaven, is rife:
  An angel comes, to stand
  With guiding lamp in hand.

There, while in darkness he adores,
Break up beneath the brazen floors;
  The graves of battles fled
  Yield all their stately dead.

Q

Nothing within us, from the sky,
May, even in its ashes, die :
    From their sepulchral urn
    Our deeds of worth return ;

Changed as the seed, that, from the mould,
Lifts its refulgent form, to **fold,**
    With kisses close imprest,
    The Summer to its breast.

O hero hearts ! where'er ye keep
Your sacred vigils, in the deep
    Death slumber of mankind,
    To faith and mercy blind ;

Whate'er the perils of the night,
The fitful, unremittent fight,
    O'er the enduring will
    A light is shining still.

'Tis that which once, through Zion's gloom,
Smote the stern warders of the tomb,
    And made the burial stone
    The God Messiah's throne.

THE BLIND SEER.

THY **guiding hand,** thou faithful friend! thy helping arm
    once more.

Thanks! now I rest upon the cliff, above the wave-worn
    shore.

I hear the merry bathers shout, upon the waters free,

And thrill, within my heart, to feel the motion of the sea.

Now read me from the Holy Page,—for I, alas! am blind,—

Of Him who came the fearful spells of darkness to unbind;

Of Him who came with words of might, to wake the buried
    will.

Why did He pass away and leave the blind to mourn Him
    still?

Pause! read no **more.** What words are these? 'according
    to thy faith

Shall be the gift that Heaven bestows:' 'tis thus the Master
    saith.

Oh! for the spiritual strength to ask and to receive.

Help Thou mine unbelief, O Lord! Thou dost, I do be-
    lieve.

The sunny billows dance and play upon the ocean's brim;

The sudden rainbows flush the waves, or melt in vapors
    dim;

The sheep, along the pleasant shore, browse o'er the grassy
    downs;

In shadow lie the forest **glades**; **in** sunshine laugh the
    towns;

With altar candles all alit, like **beadsmen** to a shrine,

In long procession march the stars, and **make** the night
    divine;

And some, they say, together move in mystic grace **with**
    them,

Like spirits of the wise, who sought the babe of Bethlehem.

I know not what a star is like, or what a flower may be.

The loveliness of human kind, alas! is not for me.

I never saw the blessed light, **that** kindles with the **morn.**

In lonely midnight I have dwelt, since, sightless, I was
    born.

Yet not for outward things I ask the miracle of grace.

Oh! could **I** see,—a moment see,—my Master's blessed
    face!

For sure am I, that **all** the rest would scarce mine eyes
    employ,

When Jesus shone, **to** flood my soul with morning beams
    of joy.

Yet no; for eighteen hundred years the Radiant One has
   fled;
And pining hearts, that call for Him, in hopeless shadow
   tread.

Friend, friend! art gone? was it thy hand that touched
   mine eyes but now?
All earth recedes: what world is this? what gifts my soul
   endow?
This is not earth, for, where I heard, but now, the solemn
   sea,
Roll rising uplands, beautiful as Heaven itself might be.
I sat upon a rugged cliff; but here a temple stands,
Paved with the ruby and the pearl, in place of ocean
   sands.
And who are these? the blossoms wave beneath them as
   they glide,
And, where they smile upon the air, the air is glorified.
And I am rising. O my heart! what swift, what sweet
   desire
Draws me to One, whose breath of life 'tis rapture to in-
   spire.
'Tis He who touched mine eyes; 'tis He awakes mine
   heart to sing.
In holy joy I kneel before my Saviour and my King.

O miracle of Love Divine!   A moment since I heard,
Through outer sense, on earth afar, the letter of the Word.
Now all the Angels chant as one, with voices of delight,
The spirit of its melodies, **as** thunders wake their might.
And it is thunder; and it **swells,** and booms, and breaks afar,
As if it were a sea, whose drops were each a vocal star.

I must return to earth again,—this is the message given,—
Blind for **a** time to outer things, but lit with sight for
     Heaven,
That so I may the more **declare,** that inner eyes and true
Are folded in the outer orbs, beyond the mortal view;
That inner eyes may even now, when Jesus, with his hand
Removes their blindness, wondrously behold the Blessed
     Land.

AN AMERICAN PICTURE.

SOLEMNLY whisper the pines, on the cliffs of the blue Adi-
     rondacks,
Heard through the gathering mist like the desolate wail of
     the ocean:
Crisped are the lilies with frost on the banks of the Schroon
     and **the** Hudson:

Autumn is stripped, by the winds, of his garment of gor-
      geous colors,
Stripped, as was Joseph **of** old, by the hands of his bluster-
      ing kinsmen.

Like an implacable warrior, advancing by night on his war-
      path,
Piercing the hearts of the foe with a cloud of invisible
      arrows,
Striking his **hatchet of steel in** the bosoms of maidens be-
      loved,
Robbing the beautiful head of its glory of odorous tresses,
Comes the pale foe from the North, from the home of the
      reindeer and sable.

Gurgle the sorrowful streams, with a sigh of lament, through
      the meadows :
Fled are the soft Summer **days,** as the deer from the shafts
      of the hunter :
Cold grows the lap of the earth, as the breast of a desolate
      woman,
Prostrate, despised and forlorn, by the snow-covered graves
      of her household.
Now, like the Prodigal Son, stands the Year shaking mast
      from the beeches,

Feeding the swine, while his tears fall in ice-drops, con-
    gealed on his bosom.

Foolish, improvident Year! he has squandered his manifold
    treasures:
Fled are the hopes of his youth, they return but in pale
    apparitions.
Flora, the beautiful, once crowned **him with** clustering
    blossoms.
Laughing Pomona rejoiced, as she fed him with fruits **in
    her orchards.**
Ceres, the bounteous, **poured at** his feet from the horn **of
    her plenty.**
Gone are the midsummer eves, when **the** fays bade him
    home to their revels.

Prodigal **Year! he** will rise from afar, and return **to his**
    Father,
Home to the Glorious Land, that he pines for in sadness
    and exile;
Welcomed, with blessings and smiles, at the feast **where**
    they eat and are merry;
Clad with the robe of **the** skies, and eternity's ring on his
    finger.

————

INDIAN SUMMER.

Now the trees put on their war paint,
Braves **and** sachems without number,
All the painted tribes of Summer
In the pleasant Northern woodlands;
For the Winter comes, the white man,
With his pale **invading** squadrons,
With **the** hoar-frost, sure and piercing
As the long knife or the rifle.

Now the flowers, the papooses,
Perish in the leafy wigwams;
Now **the** darkened clouds roll westward,
Like the flying droves of bison;
Now the sumac and the alder
Drop their red blood in the vallies;
While the tall pine, solemn chanting
On the rugged Adirondacks,—
Prophet of his fading people,—
Sings their dirge and resurrection.

I remember, pacing slowly
By **the** tranquil German Ocean,

All the days that were and are not;
How ye grew in your seclusion,
While the sweet life fed the maple;
How ye filled your cups with odors,
Sassafras and birch and cedar;
How ye whispered to the waters,
" Soon our brother will be with us,
.Yes, our brother! he is coming;
From his war-path we will greet him,—
Brother of the forest people."

Come to me, O friends and kinsmen!
From your lodges by the Hudson;
Let the west wind waft your spirit;
There is room within my bosom.
All the trees, the braves and sachems;
All the flowers, the papooses;
Maids and mothers of my people,
Bending Maize and Meadow Lily,
Rose of June and gay Spring Beauty,
Come, in tender apparitions,
With the mocassins of silence,
With the robes of sleep and shadow,
With the songs of all your fountains,
With the smile of all your waters,

With your weapons of the rainbows,
With your arrows of the sunshine
Plumed with feathers of the morning,
Feathers of the red war eagle.
We will haste upon the war-path:
Come and we will slay the Winter!

I have found him in his wigwam,
Love of self, the piercing serpent,
With his eye the massasauga,—
Traced him in his mazy pathway,
Heard him by the warning rattle.
He, the Father of the Winter,
Striking at the squaws and sachems,
At the children, the papooses!
In his fangs the icy venom,
In his breath the sleep of madness:
We will combat the Destroyer.

Come to me with sound and motion;
Breathe your love through voice and language;
Waft your fragrance through my bosom;
Till the Heart Spring smiles around me,
While the quickened souls, believing,
Feel the breath of the Wacondah,—
Welcome in the Great Good Spirit.

TO MARIE.

THE Year, upon her bridal bed,
  Of chaste December snow,
  Of white December **snow,**
Unto Eternity is wed :
In blissful trance her countenance
  Fades from our sight below.

A youthful **queen,** in Summer green,
  (**She** taught the **rose to blow,**)
  The tender rose **to blow,**
But stole **from me my Rosalie,**
  Nor soothed a mother's woe.

She stole away my golden girl,—
  The sun began to glow,—
She wrought a pinnace all of pearl,
A pinnace for my golden girl,
  The sails were white as snow.
She stole her to the Summer Isles,
A little bridesmaid, dressed in smiles,
  Before her face to go.

The Year is on her bridal bed,
　　Her couch of silver snow,
　　Of luminescent snow ;
But Rosalie she must resign,
My Rosalie, for ever mine !
My golden girl will come again,
　　Will come again I know.

————

FRIENDS IN AMERICA.

As I muse, in dusky twilight,
　　On this far but friendly strand,
All the faithful, the beloved,
　　Come, in shining robes, to stand
Like celestial apparitions,
　　From the Heart's diviner land.

There the pure affectioned maidens,
　　With the glory on their brows,
Breathing silent benedictions
　　With their consecration vows,—
To the Infinite Beloved
　　Each a saintly, child-like spouse.

There the young men, sunward moving,
   Building virtues in the day,
Led by Charity and Mercy
   Through **the** fearful spirit-fray ;
With beatitudes encompassed ;
   Clothed in **virginal array.**

Blissful wives and blooming mothers !
   Watchful fathers of the fold !
Some with locks that time has whitened ;
   All with **hearts** of love untold ;
By the Angel of **the** Churches
   On his fairest page enrolled ;—

Oh ! they **come, they come,** divested
   Of the **forms that perish here.**
They reflect a light, resplendent,
   From the Master they revere,
While He flows through all their bosoms,
   With a message full of cheer.

These, my Ministering Angels,
   Knit **by** living ties, that thrill,
As the waves of Eden flowing,

In the silent realms of Will:
Let me clasp them, let me bless them,
With a brother's blessing still.

NEW USES.

The Summer smiles, in veils of light aërial,
  Yet bids farewell to space:
Autumn, with **purple robe** and crown imperial,
  Calls to the martial race.

Farewell, O Summer! with thy lyric roses,
  Thy milk **and wine outpoured** :—
Autumn for **me** the tented field uncloses,
  I grasp the flamy sword.

Sword of the Spirit, falchion all resplendent,
    What battles shall **be** thine!
What destinies upon thy **blade** are **pendant,**
    What victories **divine!**

Whitby, Yorkshire,
    Sept. 19*th,* **1859.**